Partners Again

PARTNERS AGAIN

A story about imagination, cookies, chalk dust,
murder, blue diamonds, and family

ARTHUR T. LEE

Illustrations by
NICK BONTORNO

Nobility Publishing, P.O. Box 1338, Brush Prairie, WA. 98606

© 2009 Arthur T. Lee. All rights reserved. No part of this book may be reproduced or transmitted in any form or by any means, electronic or mechanical including photocopying, recording, or by any information storage and retrieval system — except by a reviewer who may quote brief passages in a review to be printed in a magazine, newspaper, or on the Web — without permission in writing from the publisher.

First Printing 2009
Printed and bound in the United States of America.

ISBN 13: 978-0-9802297-0-7
Library of Congress Control Number: 2008902688

Arthur T. Lee, www.arthurtlee.com

Illustrations copyright © Nick Bontorno, 2009
www.nickbontorno.com

Interior & Cover Design by Sun Editing & Book Design, www.suneditwrite.com

ATTENTION CORPORATIONS, UNIVERSITIES, COLLEGES, AND PROFESSIONAL ORGANIZATIONS: Quantity discounts are available on bulk purchases of this book for educational, gift purposes, or as premiums for increasing business. Special books or book inserts can also be created to fit special needs. For information, please contact Nobility Publishing, P. O. Box 1338, Brush Prairie, WA. 98606

To My Children

May you never become so preoccupied with life that you forget how to

IMAGINE.

*It is, after all, as simple as closing your eyes.
Sure as shootin'. For sure, for sure.*

Special thanks to:
My Lovely Wife, My Mom & Dad,
Kathryn Moss, Joseph & Andrew Price, Jessica Taylor,
Renae Southwick, Janelle Schaffner, Benjamin Machen,
the Simpson family, Sheena Davies, Sheryl Bennett,
and Jill Ronsley of *Sun Editing & Book Design*.

—**A. T. L.**

Mom & Dad—for your love and encouragement.

—**N. B.**

CONTENTS

Prologue		13
1	The Daydream	17
2	A Mob Boss	24
3	Dead Dog Crick & Blind Corners	30
4	The Secret Basement	41
5	Detention & Chalk Dust	56
6	Partners Go	63
7	Cultured Diamonds	70
8	Partners Come	80
9	For Everyone's Sake	88
10	Foul Play	92
11	Doing Hard Things	97
12	The Gateway	105
13	Don't Trust Anyone	113
14	The Legend of Joey Kornwallace	122
15	An Elementary Student's Worst Nightmare	130
16	Real Danger	136

17	Reflections	150
18	Making Wishes	157
19	Up And At 'em	163
20	The Bearded Cub Scout	167
21	The Desert Crazies	172
22	Always A Way	178
23	The Exit Interview	184
24	Light at the End of the Tunnel	190
25	The Final Struggle	194
26	A Change of Heart	200
27	The Rescue	211
28	A Partner Returns — For Good	223

Epilogue	229
Glossary	235
Come! See What's on ArthurTLee.com	239

Prologue

Summer break had ended long ago and the school year at Elderwood Elementary (the worst school in the whole world!) was now, like the pit's pendulum, in full swing.

Albert E. McTweed had advanced from the fifth grade to the sixth. From innocent fun to adult-like responsibility. From sitting in a cluster of three or four to sitting by himself in the last desk in the last row in the farthest corner from the playground. From what seemed like basic math to the terrors of square roots and Pi and other irrational numbers. To Albert, though, it all seemed irrational.

The days of two wonderfully long recesses were long gone, as were the *Friday Fun Activities* and the quarterly behavior cards with their happy plusses and not-so-happy minuses. Now, more than ever, *everything* Albert did was subject to failure; and it all seemed to be but preparation for the bigger, more terrifying stage of junior high. But while advancement to the sixth grade and earning the right to sit atop the elementary hierarchy for once should have been a milestone in his young life, it was not.

Albert was restless. His summer vacation had been the worst ever! He wished he had never left his fifth grade classroom. He wanted his old teacher back. In fact, now he wished his family had never even moved at all. He wanted *everything* to be the way it used to be.

He yearned for the good ol' days; the simple days of Arts and Crafts, when how you folded your Origami was more important than who founded which Old West town in what year and under what set of special circumstances.

History, Albert often thought, I hate it! And he did — along with Geography, English, Reading, Science, Music, Math, Spanish, P.E., and every other subject ever invented. Although it wasn't always that way. Not…last year. And not necessarily last week, either.

You see, this hatred of his was a fairly recent thing. And along with his burgeoning[1] imagination, it was propelled by a series of unexplainable problems at home; or rather problems his parents, Laura and Patrick James McTweed, were having, which Albert *simply* could not understand. Although he did try — to the point of exhaustion and bitterness.

And that is precisely where we join him now — engulfed in such a miserable state; sitting in his classroom; sketching a picture of a hatless cowboy from the very depths of his imagination onto the face of his desk. In his daydreams, he had followed his cowboy friend on many adventures. Today would be no different.

Albert leaned back to admire the drawing of his old friend. It looked good…oh, except for one thing. Albert picked up his pencil again. He almost forgot. Why, a cowboy was no good without his —.

"Students!" Ms. Hogsteen snorted, snapping at a map of the Mojave Desert with her infamous wooden pointing rod. "Here is where today's lesson begins."

Albert took one glance at the Californian desert and turned away. "I don't care," he mumbled, shifting in his seat to look outside.

Through the dreary drops of condensation on the thick, plastic classroom window, he could just make out the blurry outline of the Big Toy on the playground. It lay covered in a thick, inviting, comfy blanket of fog — perfect for wrapping oneself up in, with a hot cocoa perhaps, and daydreaming...

From behind the plains of Albert's imagination, a sun began to rise. Like a giant orange on fire, it burned its way across the periwinkle blue sky, coming to a stop at high-noon — not a minute too soon, not a minute too late.

Then a wind picked up too, breathing new life into the hundreds of tumbleweeds lounging about on the desert sands. They bumbled across the forefront of his imagination like a herd of thirsty buffalo in search of the one good water hole.

And finally, from just beyond the dunes came the terrible whir of a rusty, red, single-engine crop duster. It circled through the air like a giant metal vulture, casting its menacing shadow onto the wavering life below. On board, a struggle ensued. Words were exchanged; punches too. And then, just like that, it was over. A window opened, a body toppled out, and the plane's chatter faded back into the distance...

1

THE DAYDREAM

PJ McDougal had just enough time to think. After all, being thrown from a crop duster over the unforgiving desert of Death Valley has never really allowed for much time to do anything else but think. It hardly seemed fair. But so it was.

The wind roared like a wild lion. Hungry and violent, it tossed PJ's body to the left, then to the right, then the left again and then the right and the left and the right and so on until he felt like a pair of long johns hung out to dry.

He tried to block the wind a bit with the heels of his cowboy boots, but it was no use. It just kept coming. Water gushed from his eyes and his cheeks nearly flapped off toward the horizon. His nostrils flared real big-like, his ears whistled Dixie[2], his matted blond hair quickly un-matted, and his cowboy hat — !

PJ grabbed at the top of his head. His cowboy hat! It was missing! His eyes burned with anger. He turned them to the yellow desert below and watched in horror as the grains of sand grew bigger and bigger and bigger. The end was upon him. In just a few blinks of an eye, he was going to hit the sand, suffer brief but unbearable pain, and die a grisly death. And all without his cowboy hat.

"This is a pickle," he clamored. "For sure, for sure."

An ugly, red-beaked vulture stopped flapping its wings long enough to look PJ in the eye and envision a hearty meal a little later on.

PJ gulped. "A big, juicy pickle. Sour, too."

Shoot, thought PJ, everyone knows dying can't be seen as anything less than sour. It was what it was. But still... PJ's head shook with disappointment. To do so — to head off to the pearly gates without your cowboy hat? Why, it was unthinkable! It was preposterous! And it just plain wasn't fair.

PJ looked over his shoulder at the bright sky and shook his fist. "Might as well spit on my boots, too!"

Next to losing your hat, having your boots spat upon was about the most humiliating thing that could happen to a cowboy. And such a thing usually ended with a swift and brutal retaliation — if not from the spat-upon, then from The Great-Dueling-Deity, for sure. Because God doesn't take kindly to bad guys spitting on good guy's soles.

Once, a man with no teeth hawked a big ol' brown blob of tobacco juice all over PJ's left boot and within seconds got his *just deserts*[3]. Why, before PJ could even draw his gun, a sudden heart attack sucked the life right out of the offending party and he fell to the floor — dead — like a crispy piece of bacon sizzling in its own juices.

PJ patted the silver gun in a holster around his waist. He was the quickest draw in the west, and probably the east, too. But no one was as quick as the Golden-Spurred-Man-Upstairs. When He hangs your wanted poster up in that heavenly post office of His, you know your days are numbered.

PJ looked at his fingers, counting the seconds he had left till final touch down. *One, two, three, four...* A desperate sigh escaped his lips. *Five*. He was playing his final hand. Like a man buying a burial plot, he scanned the layout of the desert. It reminded him of the blanket he had when he was a wee cow-babe whittling his first toy gun on his momma's lap. It was big. It was yellow. It looked like it might cause some serious itching. And it had lots of critters crawling across it, too.

A couple of spotted lizards basked under the sun atop a large rock. A pack of desert coyotes scrambled into a nearby den. A rattlesnake chomped on an unlucky Kangaroo Rat. And a Gila monster, also lounging in the sun, looked up and smiled.

PJ shrugged his shoulders. No sense in not being cordial, he figured, so he kindly returned the smile before gazing heavenward. He really wished he had his cowboy hat. What on earth was he going to tell his Maker?

'Thousand 'pologies 'bout my hat, Sir. Some real bad guys beat me up. And then they took my hat. And then they *squoze* my body through some plane window — real tiny like. And then I fell to my death. So here I am. Uh... by the way, where's the saloon up here?'

A saloon. PJ licked his lips. He hadn't been in the desert but a few seconds and his lips were already chapped. He tried to swallow, but his throat was parched, too, and it hurt something fierce.

PJ slapped his leather chaps indignantly. "Boy howdy! Beats all, don't it? Why, if I don't get a good drink in me soon — at least a Sarsaparilla or two — I'm gonna die of the de-hy-dration first. For sure, for sure."

He wondered how long it would take for someone to find his body. And when they did, would he be recognizable? He wondered what everyone would say and how the next day's papers might read. Would people cry? Surely there would be a special day set aside in his honor. But would he be buried in his cowboy get-up — spurs and all? And, most importantly, for which adventure would he be remembered the most?

He hoped it wasn't this *last* adventure of his. Seems like people nowadays only ever remember the deceased for how they *went out*. At least that's how it was for his best friend. The bravest cowboy PJ ever knew. Like a father, too. Once rounded up a whole criminal posse with a single spur and a flaming bottle of whiskey.

But then, one day as he was coming out of the saloon after a little too much celebration, he stepped in a fresh pile of manure and — *whoop!* — down he went. Last thing he saw was the horse's rear end. His head hit the ground and — lights out, adios, a one-way ticket to cowboy heaven.

The paper ran a brief story entitled, MANURE STRIKES MORTAL BLOW; MANY MOURN. On his gravestone, they carved the words: FELL INTO MANURE AND DIED! And that was it. Nothing whatsoever about any of his heroic deeds. Not a single, solitary word.

Typical, PJ thought. And tragic, too. It didn't matter now, though. He would be with his old buddy soon enough, tipping back a few cold sodas for old time's sake. He hoped his friend was buying, seeing as the bad guys in the plane had robbed him of the few coins he did have right before they tossed him out the window.

PJ turned out his pockets as proof of his poverty. Below him, the individual grains of sand were beginning to take shape. A grove of Joshua trees wavered in the distance. Behind them, a graveyard of considerable size occupied an otherwise barren plot of land. And to the north of the cemetery a — a — PJ squinted to keep the wind out of his eyes — a town!

Like a flash of gold in a rusty pan of dirt, a sudden and all-encompassing surge of hope lit up PJ's insides. Had his assailants made a mistake? Instead of the middle of the desert, had they thrown him out of the crop duster prematurely — over the edge of the desert — the very edge that just so happened to border the well-known Old West town of Dead Dog Crick?

PJ's hands boomed as eager palm met eager palm. Like a pair of binoculars, his eyes focused in on the distant blur until its edges sharpened and a small town emerged — like a beacon, beckoning all to come and partake of its humble, gracious, desert hospitality.

They had made a mistake! They had! They had! They had!

PJ slapped a calloused hand over his forehead. "Shoot! I shoulda remembered. There's *always* a way out. No matter how juicy the pickle gets, there's always an escape — if you just put your mind to it." He tapped the side of his head with the tips of his fingers. "Sure as shootin'. For sure, for su —."

Ssssssss!

Like air from a balloon, a loud hissing noise burst from the sand below. Eyes as big as horse apples, PJ looked past his boots into the equally enlarged eyes of the Gila monster, who, for all intents and purposes, was not smiling anymore and would not have occasion to ever smile again.

Before PJ could say 'Holy Gila monster!' leather boots met leather hide, and a loud *splat* echoed across the desert, immediately followed by the horrific crackling of cartilage and bones. PJ's body crumpled up into a ball of red plaid and blue jeans while the Gila monster's became one with the sand. But what no one expected was the very noise that came next.

Crack!

Albert, who up until now had been staring out his classroom window, jumped into the air a good two or three feet. Heart pounding, palms sweating, he shifted his eyes to the face of his desk where shards of a familiar wooden pointing rod lay smoking across his pencil drawing of PJ McDougal.

"Albert E. McTweed!"

Ms. Hogsteen's breath moistened his face. He didn't dare look at her. He turned his eyes to the floor, but the hem of her purple muumuu and the tongues of her dirty, white sneakers glared back at him like rabid dogs. Weighing in at 350 pounds — part Gorilla, part Hippo — Ms. Hogsteen was impossible to miss.

"You weren't daydreaming again, were you? Were you?"

Albert's head whipped back and forth. He could hear the kids around him whispering and snickering. His face glowed red. He hated school. He hated his teacher. She wasn't fair. *Nothing* was. If she caught you eating paste she'd only make you stand against the wall for one recess. But if she caught you daydreaming a couple times in a row, it was straight to the principal's office — where *anything goes*.

Ms. Hogsteen waddled back to the front of the classroom. From the chalk tray, she picked up a long piece of chalk and rolled it between her fat palms. All snickering stopped. Albert shivered; his classmates, too.

"There will be no more daydreaming," she whispered threateningly. "You are here to learn. Period. Is that clear?"

It was; brutally so.

"And no drawing on your desk, either!"

Albert nodded again.

"Good." She thumped her chest, glaring at the clock. "Now, class, when you return from recess, we'll start working in your math books."

A collective groan pierced the air, but a second glimpse of the chalk in her hand put an immediate end to it. Flipping the pale piece of chalk into the air, she quickly snatched it back out of the sky like a frog would a fly. Before she could toss it into the air again, however, the room had emptied and the playground was abuzz with a catastrophic concoction of horrible rumors.

You see, on a rare occasion someone might be foolish enough to cross Ms. Hogsteen — the mean and fat teacher that she was. And on an even rarer occasion that same someone might also come off victorious against her. But no one — no one — was foolish enough to cross her (or any teacher for that matter) when she held in her chubby hands the very means by which to wipe out elementary life as the kids knew it. And chalk dust, it had long been rumored, would certainly do just that.

2

A Mob Boss

As Albert sat at the dinner table that night recapping for his parents the day's events, he could not help but feel change was on the horizon. And while change can sometimes be good, this kind was not.

His dad, wearing his traditional plaid dress shirt designed with various shades of blues shaped like diamonds, sat on one side of the table; his mom on the other. They spoke to him or through him. But that was it. A long period of silence followed. Albert sensed they were not thinking about *his* day.

"It should be...a crime," his mom started, hesitantly sharing the tender feelings of her heart. "Sales call after sales call. I mean, you see your boss more — more than you see..."

Instantly, her voice faded, but the direction to which her eyes shifted was unmistakable.

Albert looked out the window. The sun was setting; the sky darkening. His mind and heart, too. He closed his eyes...

Focusing on the black sky as it stood duplicated in his mind, he struggled to add some measure of light to the darkness setting upon them all. He concentrated as hard as he could, then harder still, until he had completely shut out the hurried whispers and the brutal, unsaid words of his parents.

From behind a lonely group of clouds in his imagination, a crescent moon finally emerged. Like a welcome nightlight, it cast its soft glow onto his house, over his yard and across the neighborhood and vacant fields, then down the main street and onto the pier where the cold ocean waters lapped at the docks like a snake sniffing out prey with every flip of its forked tongue. The docks, normally bustling with fisherman, were now quiet.

Street lamps, positioned every few feet up and down the boardwalk, lit up what the moon could not. But the boat dock remained in darkness. Having just closed up shop, the pier official turned off the office light, locked the door behind him, jumped into his car, and drove off.

Several minutes of nothing followed. But then, from the hill above, two headlights emerged from behind an abandoned building. Then two more. In a game of friendly tag, the shiny black cars zipped in and out of the shadows, into the parking lot, over the curb, and down the loading dock where they squealed to a stop.

The doors of the first car opened. Out stepped two men: the first in a tan suit and white cattleman's hat, spinning a silver-handled cane; the other in an army-green suit with night-vision goggles strapped behind his head just under a silver ponytail. In the second car, a third man sat alone in the passenger seat. Silently, he observed his men at work...

"Open the trunk."

A *click* echoed across the docks as the trunk popped open. From the back, the two men hefted a heavy gray bag and untied it. A man, beaten and gagged with a dirty handkerchief, shoved his head through the opening, struggling for air. The man with the cane cut the rag from the captive's mouth.

"*¡Por favor!*" he immediately gasped, begging for mercy. "*Por favor, por favor, por favor.*"

But the two men were not interested in the desperate pleas of a so-called traitor. Without the slightest acknowledgment, they yanked him from the bag. His feet crashed to the boards below. They were stuck in cement, its crude edges tearing at his ankles as the men dragged him toward the end of the dock.

"*¡Por favor!*" he pleaded again. "*Lo siento. Lo siento.*"

The men shook their heads. It was too late for *sorries*.

"We could've been arrested," the man with goggles barked. His voice was rough like sandpaper. "I didn't dodge bullets *during* the war," he fumed, "just to be arrested *after* it!"

The other man with the cane placed a calming hand on the shoulder of his partner. "You," he explained to the prisoner, "cost us millions of dollars." His voice, though proper, sounded like a sick baby's whimper. "You see, when the Cubans began to suspect we'd been paying them with fake diamonds we had to pay them in real ones in order to calm their suspicions. One million in *real* diamonds! *Tsk. Tsk.* And all because of your carelessness."

"But it was a mistake," the man struggled to tell them in his native tongue. And he was sorry. "Was there no room for mistakes?"

"No!" the polished perpetrator fired back. "Not in the business world. And certainly not in the underworld. Al Godón's orders, you see? You should know by now — someone always has to take the fall. This time, however, the choice was easy." He turned to his pony-tailed associate. "Let's throw him in."

"No! *¡Espera!* Please — wait!" The man in cement shoes turned to look at the boss still sitting in the black car, its bright headlights his last ray of hope. "Think of my *familia*. My *niños*." He looked back at the men holding him, searching for words they'd understand. "*¡Familia!* I — have — *familia*."

"*Tsk. Tsk.* Not for long, I'm afraid."

The man's eyes widened with fear. Tears coursed down his cheeks. "You — you leave my family alone!"

"We'll see about that," the second added gruffly. "Like he said, someone always has to take the fall."

"No," the man screamed, fighting to get loose. "No, no, no! ¡Déjeme ir! Let — me — go! Help!" He was calling for his wife, for his children — for anyone who might hear. "¡Ayúdame, mi amor!"

The two captors tightened their grips, digging their fingernails into his skin. It hurt — bad — but he was beyond pain.

"Stop struggling!" the man with the ponytail demanded. "The less you fight, the sooner it'll all be over. Assuming, that is, there's room in heaven for miscreant[4] grunts like you."

Heaven. The man stopped struggling. If this really was *the end* than there was nothing more he could do. With his wife's name clinging to the bottom of his trembling lips, he dropped his head and relaxed his shoulders. "*Te quiero, mi amor.* I — love — you."

"How nice. Shall we get this over with, then?"

Uno, dos, tres...

Splash!

Like a monster, the dark waters swallowed the man whole, leaving in his place a solitary shroud[5] of bubbles and ripples. And in the few seconds it took for the cement shoes to carry him down to the dreary depths of the ocean floor below, he found himself reduced from a husband and father to a mere memory; a memory that, like the bubbles and ripples, would all-too-easily fade.

As the two disciplinarians returned to their cars, the passenger-side window of the second car rolled down and a man clad in a pin-striped suit with a tuft of cotton pinned to his lapel looked at them with approval. His smile pushed the tips of a deep scar on his cheek up into a smile of its own.

"*Bueno.* Blue Diamond Cotton," he sang with a heavy accent. "*The Comfort of Cotton. The Elegance of Diamonds.* But if the diamonds lose their elegance someone has to be held responsible, no? We have a *reputación* to keep. *¿Verdad?*"

The men agreed.

"That's why you're the boss, Al."

"I saw too many soldiers lose the war to gangrene because of some dang bullet in their thigh. We'll cut off as many infected limbs as we need to in order to protect the heart of your operation."

Al Godon smiled again. "You, *mis amigos*, are the heart... the *corazón*." He patted his. "And seeing you work hard together does mine good. *Vayamos*."

As Godón's window rolled up, the men returned to their car. Doors slammed shut, engines roared, tires screeched, and when the last of the taillights had disappeared over the hill, the docks turned silent once again.

Back home, in his room, Albert turned out his lights and went to bed, unaware of the real trouble brewing just outside his own little world, just outside the sanctuary of his very own bedroom.

3

Dead Dog Crick & Blind Corners

Albert's dad brought the car to a stop outside the schoolyard. Leaning over, he gave his son an extra-long squeeze and kissed him on the forehead.

"Have a good day, alright?"

There was a strange look in his eye. As if he knew something Albert did not; something... sad.

"And be good," he whispered. "Alright? You help Mom out when she needs it. Okay?"

Albert said that he would try.

But if he didn't hurry, he was going to be late for school and then it would be impossible to have a good day. Because next to daydreaming and turning hallway corners blindly, being late was the worst offense any student at Elderwood Elementary could commit. He had seen kids severely punished for less. And with a teacher like his there was no telling what punishment awaited him — in or out of the ring; but probably in.

It was no secret to the students that Ms. Hogsteen moonlighted as a professional wrestler in the Heavy-Heavy Weight Division of the World Wrestling Association. That was the rumor, at least, but everyone knew it was pretty much true. She was *The Hungry Hippo*, all right, former *Champion of the Wooorld*. Sure as shootin'. For sure, for —

Brrriiing.

Albert's eyes filled with terror. "No," he groaned. "I'm going to be late!"

His dad tried to give him another hug, but Albert hadn't the time. Without even a goodbye, he sprang from the car, slamming the door behind him. Like a horse on the open frontier, he raced across the yard then around the corner and onto the playground.

Kids ran back and forth, skipping rope, bouncing balls, and all together having a good time as they slowly fell into formation outside their classroom doors and waited for their teachers to let them in. Hopeful, Albert's eyes panned over to the blue door of his classroom, room number D-15. D as in *Dead* meat. The line was gone. The door was closed. And all the way from across the playground, Albert could see a familiar large blob of purple standing at the front of the room. His teacher was taking roll!

Like a rocket, Albert blasted past the Big Toy, up to his classroom, and through the cold metal door. Not bothering to hang up his coat or backpack, he skidded across the dusty, green floor and into his chair.

Maybe she hadn't called his name yet, he hoped. Maybe she didn't even notice he was late. Maybe, he thought, just maybe she wouldn't even care.

But she did. No sooner did Albert feel the hard plastic chair against his backside than Ms. Hogsteen stopped writing and lifted her sagging triple chin. Her meaty nose sniffed the air like a walrus would its pail of fish.

"Mr. McTweed," she said sternly. "You're late."

He wanted to explain, but nothing came out. His mouth was too dry from running. She wouldn't care that his dad wanted to spend a little extra time with him this morning anyway.

"We start early," she reminded the class in her snide tone, "so you can learn early. Today, I'm going to cram the sixth grade into your puny brains if it kills me." She paused, a snort rumbling from the back of her nose. "Probably will kill me," she added with another snort. "But you'll thank me for it when you're older. And why? Because you'll be smarter than all of your idiot friends outside skipping rope!"

Albert watched as Ms. Hogsteen waddled over to the maps again and slapped the west coast with a new wooden pointing rod. He imagined she had an endless supply of rods hidden somewhere in the school; a terrible room filled clear to the ceiling.

"Now quit your gawking," she shouted, rapping her pointer over the corner of a nearby desk, "and get out your Geography books!"

Out of fear, every one grabbed their books from the insides of their desks and turned to the appropriate page: AMERICA'S DESERTS: MOJAVE DESERT PART II.

"The Mojave Desert," she began reading from the first paragraph in a dull, monotone reading voice, "is located in the southwestern United States and is composed of Death Valley…"

Albert turned his eyes to the clock. In time with her unbearable drawl, the second hand ticked away the precious moments of his life. He watched it go round and round and round until a whole fifteen minutes had passed! But when he looked back at her, she was still going at it. A slimy strand of spittle stretched from the top to the bottom of her sausage-like lips, which opened and closed with no sign of letting up. Would she never stop?

Albert didn't know how much more of this he could take. He wanted to yell for her to shut up. He wanted to run up to her and stick a handkerchief in her mouth. He squeezed his temples. He covered his ears. How was he supposed to like school when it was so boring?

Albert grabbed a pencil from his bag. He imagined PJ never had to go to school when he was a kid. And look how he turned out, he thought; saving the day practically every single day; not afraid of anyone or anything. Why, he was the best and bravest of them all and there wasn't a living person who could stop him. Especially not some overweight teacher/wrestler dragging on about the importance of deserts in the world.

Before Albert knew it, the tip of his pencil had sketched the outline of the man in question in the margin of his school book. He cast a glance to the side to make sure no one was watching, then drew the cowboy a hat and tinted his chin with a little-more-than-usual scruff. Albert placed his pencil down and smiled. It was probably the best he had ever drawn. It looked so ... so real. And just like that, his imagination made it as if it was really so ...

PJ moaned. With great effort, he lifted his body from the ground and took to his knees. Blinking the sand from his eyes, he looked at the sky from where he had fallen. He patted his body from his head down to his toes. He pinched his arm — real hard. And then, he shouted for joy. "Yeeeehaw!" He was alive! It was a — a miracle. There *was*, indeed, *always* a way out.

Wasting no time, PJ jumped to his feet and looked toward the town he had seen from the air. It lay hidden behind a series of sand dunes, but he knew it was there — he could smell it, like dirty socks and ... PJ pointed his nose upward and drew in a deep breath.

"Sarsaparilla!" he gleamed. "For sure, for sure."

He could practically taste that drink of his now. Panting like a thirsty dog, he wiped the drool from his bottom lip. He paused. As if he were feeling his face for the very first time, his hand slid down his chin and across each side of his jaw, hovering over an abnormally long and uneven patch of whiskers sprouting like weeds.

Strange, he thought. He didn't remember having a beard back in the plane. He pulled at it to make sure it was real. It was. Perhaps then, he guessed, the desert air had increased the rate at which his whiskers grew. Or maybe, he speculated further, the desert sand had something to do with it. Yes, he nearly shouted. That's it! He had stumbled upon, or rather fallen into Mother Nature's highly guarded secret home remedy for male-pattern baldness!

As quick as a rattlesnake's bite, PJ's hand shot from his side, scooped up a handful of burning hot sand, and tossed it into his face. He waited for his hair to grow even more... and waited... and waited. But to his disappointment — and the future disappointment of beardless, bald men everywhere — nothing happened.

"Well, shoot," he said as he shook the sand from his whiskers. "At least I tried." Brushing a few grains from his eyebrows, he ran his fingers through his — his hat? With an air of even greater surprise than was yielded by the discovery of his beard, PJ removed a brand-spanking new cowboy hat from the top of his head.

"Well, I'll be darned."

He thought he'd lost his hat. In fact, he had lost it — around the time he was thrown out of that rusty crop duster. But now, here it was, on his head, just like it had been there the whole time. And there was no way in heck any desert air or yellow sand had anything to do with its sudden re-appearance.

"No sir," PJ admitted with a gracious tip of his hat toward the blue sky, "there is definitely a higher power behind it all. A much higher power."

With a smile as bright as the sun, PJ fastened his hat back over his sandy locks and began his trek toward Dead Dog Crick. It was then, however, no more than one step into his journey, that he noticed the Gila monster that had broken his fall; or rather the unfortunate beast whose slimy remains clung to the heavy heels of his boots.

"Poor devil." PJ scraped his boots over the sand. "That was a *Gila*-of-a thing to do, softenin' my landin' and all. Why, shoot, sacrificin' your life for a cowboy's is 'bout the noblest thing anyone... or *thing* can do."

PJ remembered back to his very first horse (a sleek mustang named Red) and the time it up and knocked him down during the middle of a much-anticipated high-noon showdown with a terrible gang of masked bandits. At first, PJ had gotten real mad. Couldn't figure out why on earth his horse would knock him to the ground like that, especially in front of a group of infamous criminals. But then he saw it: a dark trickle running down its velvety hide. The old mustang had taken one of the bad guy's bullets. It was meant for him. But Red took it on his behalf — and willingly so. It was the ultimate act of unselfishness; an eternal sacrifice fueled by love.

"Sure as shootin'," PJ sniffled back the memory as he bid a final farewell to the Gila monster. "For sure, for sure."

Speaking of horses... He really wished he had a horse with him right now. Oh well, he shrugged his shoulders, reckoning it wouldn't have fit through the crop duster window anyway. What was done was done. And there was no use crying over what you couldn't change.

And so with a click of his spurs, PJ once again began his enthusiastic trek toward the borders of Dead Dog Crick. After what seemed like hours later, though, it was all PJ could do to even pick up his feet. The wind was brutal; the sun, torturous; and the desert sands, downright unbearable.

PJ slapped his thigh. Would it ever end? He wiped his brow with the back of his hand, but it was as he feared. Not a single hint of sweat. He had sweated his last drop more than an hour before. He knew it had been his last because, at the time, his body didn't want to let go of it. He had to flex his forearm real tight-like just to push it out. But even after it had popped from his pore, it just hung there, clinging to a single hair like a stubborn drop of dew on a blade of grass, until finally, like magic, it vanished and a small puff of steam replaced it.

PJ looked to the sky like a beggar to a stingy rich man. "Gosh dang you barren skies!" He wished the desert could take on the form of a man, so he could challenge him in a duel and fight him gun to gun. But deep down inside PJ knew it was no use getting all worked up over something as unalterable as the desert. It was what it was. There would be no fight. And there certainly would be no rain.

As deep in depression as in sand, PJ trudged ahead, flakes of dry skin crumbling from his chapped cheeks onto his red plaid shirt. His lips looked leprous. His tongue felt like an old shoe. And he was pretty sure if he didn't get that good drink in him soon, the *desert crazies* would have him for lunch.

And every desert-goer knows there's no escaping the *desert crazies* once they get a hold of you. Why, they thrive on driving men to the very edge of insanity — even great cowboys like Patrick James McDougal. Because the *desert crazies* don't care who you are... or who your father was. They're rough and tough and meaner than the meanest schoolyard bully times a hundred. And sure as shooting, if you so much as underestimate *them* by one degree, they'll have you shoveling sand into your mouth like it's a tall glass of freshly squeezed lemonade. And for a minute or two, the sand might even taste like lemonade because that's how the *crazies* work. So you keep shoveling and the hot sand keeps tumbling down your throat; and when you look up next there might be a bevy of the most beautiful cowboys and cowgirls you ever laid eyes on all frolicking about in their vintage bathing suits and cowboy hats in an icy pool of water.

'Come on in,' they laugh, playfully splashing each other. 'The water feels — wonderful!' the girls add with a flirtatious giggle or two. 'Hurry,' they twitter with a smile. Then they wink and wave and it makes your head spin.

So what do you do? You kick off your boots, your chaps, your plaid, your handkerchief, and your trusty cowboy hat, and dive right in — long johns and all.

Because heck, who in their right mind would ever turn down a personal invitation to a pool party in the middle of the desert? Especially from such an alluring clique of cow-folk.

And just like that, you proceed to bury yourself in the sand, laughing and splashing and smooching your time away until right when you think it can't get any better — it doesn't.

Crack!

"Albert E.!" Ms. Hogsteen shoved her pig-like nose into his face. Her eyes burrowed into his mind like tics on a dog's back. "Strike two. One more time," she threatened, "and I'll have you serving detention under The Colonel's watchful eye."

Everyone in the room gasped. Detention was the last thing in the world anybody wanted — whether they knew it or not. And it was the last thing you would ever wish upon anyone — whether you knew them or not. Because Charlie Klinger was the worst principal ever. Like a giant ruler, he had a sharp edge to him; and he lived to cut you down if and *when* you failed to measure up.

But scariest of all to the students, Klinger was a veteran of war. Decked out in his old army fatigues with a long silver ponytail dangling from the back of his head, he patrolled the halls like a vicious guard dog, daring the lazy kids of the school to race around a corner and onto his turf, into his foxhole. Because when they did, he'd be ready for them.

He'd yank them up by the scruff of their neck like a rabbit fit for stew. "Miss Maple!" he'd yell, half spitting in her face.

"Turning blind corners here is a precursor to certain instability in the future. I didn't dodge bullets for you to be lazy. Now shape up!"

As a natural reaction, the offending-student's body would then begin to shake as if the San Andreas Fault[6] ran clean through them. Their cheeks would burn with embarrassment and they'd turn their eyes to the floor, mumbling an apology.

"I can't hear you!" he'd shout back in his boot-camp voice. "Let me remind you I was a colonel before I was a principal and I will be addressed in the order my rank was determined. Is that clear, soldier?"

Like every frivolous rule in the school, it was; frightfully so.

"I still can't hear you!"

"Yes! Colonel! Principal! Klinger! Sir!"

Ms. Hogsteen saluted the air as if The Colonel Principal were right in front of her.

"And you know exactly what The Colonel has naughty kids like you do in detention. Don't you?"

She pulled a long piece of chalk from a concealed pocket on the front of her muumuu and placed its tip against Albert's cheek.

He didn't dare move. Petrified with fear, he watched out of the corner of his eye as she slowly scraped it down his skin. The girl next to him almost threw up. The boy in front of him did, but somehow managed to swallow it back down. The classroom was as quiet as a cemetery. There was only one thing that could make detention with the principal more terrifying than it already was.

"Chalk dust," Ms. Hogsteen sneered. "Principal Klinger likes the school's chalkboards clean. He has lots of them — lots and lots and lots of them — and they are all covered with layers and layers of chalk dust."

Only the recess bell succeeded in drowning out Ms. Hogsteen's maniacal laughter. But her students weren't sticking around to hear it, anyway. In a flash, they burst onto the playground, chittering and chattering about the near-death-experience of a boy in their class.

Having lived it, Albert hurried across to the swings, where, lately, he had been spending a lot of his recess time. They were a good place to think. But there was really only one thing on his mind now. Somehow he had to learn to control his daydreams. It was as if his life depended on it.

4

THE SECRET BASEMENT

The end-of-recess-bell sounded. As if under a spell from the perilous pied piper himself, kids everywhere ran into their classrooms to take their seats.

"Class!" A puff of steam exploded from each of Ms. Hogsteen's nostrils. Her eyes darted back and forth, counting the kids as they filed into her room. "Recess is over," she barked again. "Now stop the chatter, sit down, and get out your English books. It's grammar time."

As Albert slid into his seat, he could not help but wonder what his dad was doing. He was taking the day off from BLUE DIAMOND COTTON, INC., where he worked as "the greatest cotton clothes salesman this side of the M-i-ss-i-ss-i-pp-i. For sure, for sure!" Or so he boasted every chance he got. Sometimes — just to make Albert laugh — he'd even jump onto the table, extend his arms like a carnival showman, and yell it at the top of his lungs.

Sometimes — before they moved — Albert used to go with his dad to work. But not now. Now, it was too far away. So far away, in fact, his dad had to leave before Albert was awake. And lots of times he didn't even get home till he was already in bed. Albert's mom didn't like that. Albert didn't, either. On those nights he just lay in bed daydreaming about old times.

Blue Diamond could be a boring place to spend a summer day (especially if you were a kid), but somehow his dad always found a way to make it fun for Albert. During breaks they would run around pretending co-workers were bad guys. And at lunch they'd sneak downstairs and imagine they were hiding in a secret basement. They'd overhear hurried conversations, foil sinister plots, and save the world from inevitable destruction time after time after time — until, of course, it was time for his dad to go back and "work for real this time."

When that happened, Albert usually waited in the Bronco where he often imagined all of the warehouses and buildings away until there was nothing but desert around him, or sometimes a lone dirt road crowded by run down saloons and gun shops and cemeteries and things.

Albert placed his English book on his desk and flipped it open to the appropriate page. In his head, he quoted the cotton company's famous tagline. He had heard it over the radio at least a thousand times. *'Blue Diamond Cotton. The Elegance of Diamonds. The Comfort of Cotton.* We hope to see you *there* in our cotton comfort *wear*.' Albert always changed the last part to underwear, though. He liked it better that way. His dad admitted he did too, but only when Albert's mom wasn't listening.

Once, Albert walked up and down the office shouting the new and improved slogan as loud as he could. But the boss got kind of mad and told his dad Albert had to stay out in the hallway until their special meeting was over. So Albert walked the halls, his cheeks still burning with embarrassment and anger.

At the end of the hallway, nailed to the walls on each side, were pictures of the hundreds of Blue Diamond employees. They all looked mean and grumpy — like they didn't really want to be there — and they stared out of their Polaroid imprisonments like criminals on a WANTED poster.

At the time, the creative wheels inside Albert's head began to turn. For each employee, he concocted a personality, a background and story, and a series of crimes carried out against humanity with exactness and greed. From the depths of his imagination, like steam wafting from a pot of boiling water, a world of deceit and intrigue emerged. And before Albert knew it, time, as it so often did, had passed him by.

The clock struck five. Employees everywhere were pushing in their chairs and walking away. Albert ran back to his dad's desk as fast as he could, but when he got there his dad was nowhere to be seen. His desk was clean, his computer off, and his chair pushed in. For a second, Albert began to panic. He thought his dad had gone home and — and forgotten him. But he hadn't.

"Not a chance!" he called out to Albert as he stepped out of the room where the special meeting had been held. "Partners don't leave partners behind, right?" Albert nodded. "And you and me — we're partners."

Partners. Albert reached back into his desk and pulled out his Geography book instead of his English one. Pages flew past his vision until he found the chapter on deserts from the day before. He looked at the drawing of the cowboy. The margin below had room to spare.

He looked up at Ms. Hogsteen. Her back was to the class. As fat as a hippo's, it blocked the entire chalkboard. She was mumbling something about proper grammar and rules the students should never ever break — like beginning a sentence with *And*.

Albert sighed. There were too many rules. Mindlessly, his fingers found his pencil. A slash here, a couple of dots there, a little bit of shading everywhere... Albert closed his eyes, adding in his mind the final piece of the puzzle; a splash — a very large splash — of imagination. And just like that...

"Whooee!" The arid landscape rushed past PJ's face. It felt good to be on a horse again. Now, he wasn't really sure how he had come to be on the horse, but he wasn't really going to complain, either. A horse was a horse, of course. "Sure as shootin'. For sure, for sure." Even if it didn't come with its usual saddle.

PJ grabbed at his hindquarters and grimaced. He could feel his posterior bruising as he bounced up into the air, landing hard over the bareback of his trusty steed.

Had he a long journey ahead of him, he would have scavenged the desert for some sagebrush to use as extra padding, but at this pace, he sensed the trail to the saloon was just about over. PJ licked his lips. He'd have that tall glass of Dead Dog's finest in his hands soon enough. Why, he could practically taste it already. It was sweet... real sweet.

"Yaw!" PJ dug his spurs into the ribs of his bronco and together they flew down a sand dune, leaving a trail of dusty air in their wake. They raced up and down several more dunes until, passing the grove of Joshua trees, they came upon the graveyard of considerable size, which, to their surprise, was considerably larger than it had appeared to be from 300 feet in the air.

PJ's horse skidded to a stop, dancing in place. PJ patted its thick neck as if to say 'it'll be okay', but his shaking hands and rattling boots said otherwise. As his eyes gazed over the sea of headstones before him, he couldn't help but reflect back on the infamous past that was Dead Dog Crick's and would be forever. It is a hard thing to shake a reputation — good or bad — but especially bad. And Dead Dog Crick had rightfully been branded with a bad one. Like a heavy ball and chain, that reputation followed it everywhere.

You see, Dead Dog Crick was known for one thing and one thing only: crime. In its life, it had harbored some of the greatest outlaws in all of history, offering a sort of unsanctioned sanctuary for men *and* women of all demeanors and specialties. Dead Dog was not one to judge, though. But only because it had no judge. It was the one place where the law could not touch the people. But only because there was no law.

Now, that is not to say the law did not try because it did. It was just never successful — that's all. Fact of the matter is, only a couple of weeks before, a God-fearing, law-abiding, well-mannered attorney by the name of Thaddeus P. Zookenowski left his brother Bartholomew T.'s East Coast practice to "try and bring law and order so help me God to Dead Dog Crick and it's *inhabitants*." Although "barbarians" was the actual word he used, which no one could really blame him for and, in fact, raised their celebratory glasses of bubbly to.

PJ gave a light tug on his horse's mane, bowing its head. Against his better judgment, he leaned over and scraped a pile of dust from the base of an old wooden grave marker.

<pre>
      Billy Reeds
     Frank McCloud
     Tommy Clayton
       MURDERED
      on the streets of
        Dead Dog
          1884
</pre>

Murdered? At the very thought, a shiver—like a mouse—scurried down PJ's spine and back into the desert. Swallowing the lump in his throat, he led his horse in front of a second marker. Magnified through the cloudy glass of a pile of old whiskey bottles, he could just make out the pinewood memorial.

<pre>
         Tex Busby
  Takn frim Jonson Hidout an Hangd
         Jun 16 1886
</pre>

Real uneasy-like, PJ loosened the white handkerchief about his neck. He didn't want to read another inscription. Not a single one. No, he thought, not even that one right over there. He turned his head to look away, but within seconds felt it turning back. The capstone was calling to him…

"Ahhh, shoot!" PJ gave in and rode up to the gravestone. A steer skull sulked in front of it. "Yesterday," he read. "Thad—." He stopped. "Yesterday?" He wiped a nervous sweat from his mouth, reading on, sounding out the strange name immortalized in stone. "Tha-deuss P. Zoo-ken-owski. Attorney-at-Law.

Guilty —." He stopped again, but this time to catch his fleeting breath before continuing to read aloud what his eyes had regretfully glanced ahead to see. "Guilty of carryin' out the law. Beaten up, dragged away by horses, then—then left for the coyotes and buzzards to pick him clean?"

A terrifying picture flashed across the minds of both PJ and his horse. Spooked, his horse bucked once. PJ grabbed on to its mane. It bucked twice. PJ grabbed onto its ears. It bucked a third time.

"Whoa!" he shouted. "Whoa!"

But the bronco wouldn't be consoled. Like a silver bullet, it bolted ahead, trampling grave marker after grave marker, unearthing old skeletons like a plow horse overturning dirt. Helpless, PJ hunkered down for the bumpy ride. A sign filled with bullet holes whizzed past him.

> Welcom to Dead Dog Crick
> wher the safes place be in the ground.
> Pop-you-lay-shun: one les than
> ther wer ye'terday

It was the most unfriendly welcome sign PJ had ever had zip by him. And it sure as heck didn't make him feel very welcome. He looked behind him as the sign and the town's border turned into a distant memory. His horse, however, was in no hurry to make any more memories like that. Putting on the brakes, he sent PJ sprawling through the air once again.

It seemed PJ's lot in life to make crash landings on desert floors. His eyes scanned the ground for any fresh piles of manure—because this was no place to end up like his friend. Thankfully, the coast was clear.

"Umph!" PJ slammed into the ground, a cloud of dirt instantly souring his mouth. Like a horseshoe in a sandpit, he skidded past the stores cluttering Dead Dog's main street: *Cody Pucket's Boot and Saddlery*, *The Moonlight Barbershop*, and *Pace*

Johnson's Gun, Coffin & Everything Store. A sign just outside the window of the latter advertised the new arrival of *The Gentleman Six-Shooter*.

> For certain to put the man you want
> in the coffin you want.
> Buy a gun and coffin,
> get a FREE cigar.

Across the street, smoke rose from a recently-burned-down lawyer's office. A HELP WANTED sign flapped back and forth in what used to be the window. Someone had scribbled in the word **NO** before the word HELP.

PJ looked away, sickened by the brutality lurking behind every sign. He was beginning not to like this place. And as he slowed to a stop, he couldn't help but wonder if perhaps he should have stayed in the desert. Because *there*, his enemies were as clear as day to him: the sun, the snakes, the buzzards, and the desert crazies — that's all. There, he knew what to watch for. But *here*...

PJ covered his eyes as he slid past an overturned stage coach with the skeletal remains of the unlucky driver hogtied to a front wheel. Here, he had no clue who or what he might be up against. Was it really worth it? Risking his life for a cold drink?

"Ugh!" PJ groaned again as his head rammed into a set of rickety stairs. He struggled to his feet. A two-story shack with a heavy set of swinging doors occupied the space in front of him. Like a period at the end of a sentence, it marked the end of the main street and the end of PJ's quest. From inside, the sweet smell of the hard stuff penetrated his dirt-clogged nostrils, causing him to forget any of his previous concerns about Dead Dog, its peoples, and, of course, its signs.

PJ took one step backwards so as to read in its entirety the fancy lettering across the building's façade. "Wild Willy's Motel and Saloon. Home of the—." He smiled. "Ce-lestial Saloon Girls." Yes, he had definitely reached his destination. "For sure, for sure."

Puffing out his chest, he toed the threshold, gripped the tops of the saloon doors and swung them open. "Ladies," he called out with great swagger. "Don't crowd me all at once now. There's plenty of time to take a drink with each and every one of you."

But to PJ's dismay, there were no girls. His brow descended. His bottom lip curled. In fact, the saloon was as barren as that there desert behind him. He stepped further into the dark room to have a look around. Strange, he thought. Everything looked as it should be. There were chairs and tables and a bar. And bottles of whiskey too; hundreds of them even, covering the back wall like trophies on a mantle piece. But there were no customers. Where, PJ wondered, was the bartender? Where were all the unsavory patrons? Where were the spittoons? The cigars? And the one-eyed card players? The toothless drunks? And the fat piano man? And the saloon girls? Why, where in the heck was his Sarsaparilla?

Thinking the help might be in back, PJ stepped up to the bar and was just about to yell out a 'Hello? Anyone here? You have a customer up front!' when a sudden and mysterious bout of loud laughter roared from somewhere behind the bar; a somewhere that upon further inspection proved to be a well-hidden cellar door in the floor. Careful not to make any noise, PJ lifted the hatch a few inches and looked in. A lantern's light flickered from a large room at the bottom of the stairs.

PJ's eyes lit up with excitement. "A secret basement." He opened the door an inch or two more and leaned in closer. He could hear several people talking. They were holding some kind of meeting. PJ beamed again. "A secret meeting."

Like a desert mouse, he tip-toed down the stairs until he could just see the people in the room.

Unaware of the stranger on the stairs, a man in a tan suit jumped to his feet. He whipped off a white Stetson, loosened his string bow-tie, and shook a silver-handled cane in the air. To PJ's surprise, his English was polished and proper.

"What are we making fake diamonds for then, I ask, if we do not plan on buying out every country? We have no choice," he said, rapping his cane over the table. "I vote for an immediate increase in production. We have the connections. We certainly have the money. *He* can get more *ingredients* for us, I am sure of it. Now, if we're all in agreement, I will let Al Godón and the others know."

PJ listened with piqued interest. Fake diamonds? Al Godón? The others? He had heard of this Al Godón before. He was the most wanted criminal of all time. But he was also the most slippery. No one had ever caught him. In fact, no one had ever really seen him and they probably never would. The location of his hideout was one of the great unsolved mysteries of all time.

A fat man with fat lips and hair like a scorched sage brush seconded the motion of the first. "I agree with Wild Willy." His deep voice rattled as if he were under water. After balancing a black derby on his head, his hands fell to the trumpet mouthpiece dangling from a gold chain about his neck.

Next to him, a wild-eyed, red-haired man with a moustache and puffy sideburns — at least eight feet tall and ugly as sin — jumped to his feet and drew his gun. *The Gentleman Six-shooter*. He spun it on his finger this way and that then parked it in his holster and sat down.

"Then let's vote all-ready!" Like a kettle over an open flame, his face burned with impatience. "I's still got myself a lawyer's funeral to attend. An' I's a need to pick up my free *cee-gar*, too."

A funeral … for a lawyer? The last of the terrible gravestones from the cemetery leaped back into PJ's mind. Thaddeus P. Zookenowski, the man who only yesterday had nearly been dragged to death by horses and left behind as buzzard food. PJ looked into the fiery eyes of the freakish brute with sideburns. So *he* was the murderer behind it, eh?

"Well," PJ whispered to himself, "no one takes down one of the law's finest on my watch and gets away with it."

Quietly, he reached for the black handle of his gun. But then something strange happened. PJ's hand retracted. And stranger still, his heart softened. For some reason, he couldn't bring himself to grab his gun and pull the trigger as he had so often done in defense of truth and justice and all things good. In fact, he couldn't even remember why he was going to make the big oaf *dance* in the first place. Out of all the things he had once known or, at least, thought he knew, the only thing now occupying his thoughts was that never in his entire life had he seen anyone more mesmerizing than she, the woman at the head of the table.

Hair as dark as night, skin as delicate as rose petals, she wore a ruffled, red and black dress of sorts covered in sequins; and every time she moved they twinkled like the very stars in the heavens. Her lips were soft, her cheeks rosy, and her nose petite. And her eyes? Oh, her eyes, her eyes, her eyes! They were big and bright and —

"Beautiful."

PJ slapped a trembling hand over his mouth. He didn't mean to say it; the word had just slipped out. But he did mean what he said — every syllable. Why, he couldn't take his eyes off her. She *was* too "beautiful," he said again. "Beautiful, beautiful, beaut — !"

"Albert!" a classmate screamed. "Watch out!"

Sheer terror seized Albert's face. Oh no! He had been daydreaming — again! A terrible growl rumbled from across the room. And *she* — the fat, purple hippo — had seen him!

A heavy shadow fell over Albert's desk. A blur of purple consumed his vision. Grabbing his chin, her clammy hands forced his gaze from his desk to her face, moistened by beads of sweat. Her nostrils flared. Like a giant earthworm, her tongue wet her lips. Albert's worst nightmare was about to come true.

"Please don't wrestle me," he whimpered, closing his eyes as if for protection. "Please."

"What?" Ms. Hogsteen laughed. "I'm not going to wrestle you. I promise."

But Albert knew she was lying. He opened his eyes. Like a painting under the rain, her purple muumuu morphed before his imagination until it was a fantastic spandex wrestling suit. Her silver hair disappeared, too, and a hat made to look like a hungry hippo with a silver Mohawk and sharp, blood-stained fangs took its place. Ms. Hogsteen rubbed her fat belly and growled her infamous growl.

"Let's go!"

"Now?"

"Now!"

Like a whale on a trampoline, she lunged into the air, her fat fingers zeroing in on Albert's fragile neck.

"No!" he screamed. "Noooo!"

But it was too late. *The Hungry Hippo* grabbed him by the right arm and twisted him into the shape of a pretzel. It was her signature move. The dreadful *Super Deadly Death Grip of Power*!

"Let go of me." Albert kicked her in the shin as hard as he could, causing her to relax her grip. Free for the moment, he scurried across the mat.

Boo! Boo! Boo's! flooded the arena

Albert looked up, sick to his stomach. He was surrounded. Hundreds of thousands of people loomed in front of him; a national wrestling arena filled to capacity; a blood-thirsty crowd of faculty members — their thumbs down; their voices raised; screaming for his utter destruction.

"Fee. Fi. Fo. Fum."

Ms. Hogsteen whirled around, licking her chops. She was going to chew him up like a piece of gum (even though she knew there was no gum allowed in class). She was going to catch him and beat him and tear him apart him limb from limb.

Albert panicked. There was nowhere to run. There was nowhere to hide.

Whooosh!

The Hungry Hippo dove for him. Forced by circumstance, Albert ducked and scrambled under her legs, running to the far corner; to the ropes; to the referee. But his opponent wasn't but a step behind him.

Whooosh!

She spun around and lunged at him again, her fat arms thrashing the air.

Albert raised his hands in defense. But it was no use. She was too fast. In an instant, his world appeared upside down. Like a cat toying with a mouse, she dangled him by his right foot.

The crowd jumped from their chairs, cheering and booing at the same time. They threw popcorn and trash into the ring. Their pointer fingers sliced back and forth across their necks. They were chanting something...

"End it now! End it now! End it now!"

"Finish it," a janitor shouted.

"Tear his arms off," a recess lady yelled.

The Hungry Hippo grunted her approval. Releasing Albert's foot, she grabbed his arm and squeezed. It hurt — bad. She swung him around and around and around. Life was passing him by, but he couldn't stop it. He was getting dizzy, then dizzier still. Finally, her grip relaxed and Albert felt his body flying through the air. He sailed over the ropes and the crowd and toward a door. Without hands, it opened and he tumbled through it and into the —

The school hallway?

Albert opened his eyes to see an exhausted Ms. Hogsteen towering in front of him. Her face was as purple as her muumuu; her eyes as angry as his.

"Why," she breathed heavily, "do you," she wheezed, "have to be," she choked, "so difficult?"

She looked deep into her pupil's eyes, searching. But Albert wasn't going to tell her anything. He hated her. He hated this school. He hated — everything! That's why he was *so difficult* — whatever that meant. Because he was mad. Okay? He was mad. At everything!

Ms. Hogsteen shook her head. That was no excuse. "To the principal's office," she said. "Now!"

5

DETENTION & CHALK DUST

Principal Klinger led the march from his office to the ignominious[7] detention room. Albert and two others trailed close behind in a single-file line.

"Pick up those feet, soldiers!" Klinger yelled. "I dodged bullets so you could be productive. Not lazy. I'm on a schedule. Now move, move, move!"

As commanded, Albert and the others picked up the pace.

A scrawny, red-haired kid with freckles tapped Albert on the shoulder. "What are you here for?"

Albert looked at the floor in embarrassment. He didn't dare say he had been caught daydreaming in class.

"Swearing," he whispered. "The real bad words. You?"

"Sniffing markers," the red-head boasted with an overly-giddy smile, "I can still smell 'em, too. Strawberry. Grape." He took in a deep breath. "Oh yeah. And black licorice. My teacher has all kinds."

Albert crumpled his brow in despair. All he had done was close his eyes. Was he really as bad as the marker-sniffers?

The pretty girl at the end of the line chimed in. "That's nothing," she said, dismissing the boys' claims. "Klinger got me for turning a corner too fast. He patrols the hallways, you know?"

They did.

"Miss Maple!" Like an owl, Principal Klinger's head turned completely around. "No talking!"

As punishment, he increased the pace of their march until they were practically running. The student's struggled to keep up. They zigzagged in and out of secret doorways, through abandoned classrooms, and down a series of dark hallways, each one being darker than the previous. After what seemed like hours, Klinger finally stopped.

"Ten hut!"

They were *there*—the back corner of a very, very dark hallway. Miss Maple, the freckle-faced kid, and Albert huddled together. In front of them loomed a secret room, marked by a cryptic placard hanging from a rusty nail.

> NO STUDENTS BEYOND THIS POINT!
> UNLESS ESCORTED BY A FACULTY MEMBER.
> OFF-LIMITS! STAY AWAY! KEEP OUT!

A skull and cross bones glared out from under the words like a corpse from its grave.

Albert cringed. What atrocities awaited them on the other side of the door were beyond his will to imagine. He hoped it wasn't chalk dust like Ms. Hogsteen had threatened. But he knew *nothing* was beyond Principal Klinger. The sixth graders told stories about him; about the things he would do; about the things he *had* done. Some kids dismissed them as rumors; terrible, terrible rumors designed to scare the most naive. But

Albert knew otherwise. The stories were true, all right; every last one of them.

Like the one about Klinger's first birthday when he took out his old man for giving him a doll instead of plastic army men. But the *judge* appointed to the case said there was "no way in heck a 1-year old can pull this here trigger" (even though his fingerprints were all over the gun), so he released the child without the slightest form of reprimand.

Then there was the story from when Klinger was three and he got rid of his old woman, too. Her car brakes just *went out*. "Because no way in heck," the same judge declared, "can a three-year old tamper with brakes" (even though his fingerprints were all over them). "Mere coincidence," he later added. And with that his gavel fell. "Case dismissed."

An icy cold coursed through Albert's veins as he remembered back to the first time he'd heard these stories. It was tradition for the sixth graders to pass them on to the lesser grades — since they'd been around longer and seen things the others hadn't. The stories, they said his first day at Elderwood, had to be told during recess…in the bathroom…with the lights out. And if you turned around three times the glowing images of Klinger's parents would appear in the mirror. But Albert got no more than one and a half turns in before he bolted out the door, too afraid to finish the job.

"Albert!" Principal Klinger shouted. "Get in here and sit down."

Albert snapped to attention. The door in front of him was open. Inside, a heavy, black curtain divided the room in two. A row of old desks huddled against the back wall like comrades in enemy camps. The boy and girl had long since taken their seats.

"On the double, soldier!"

Klinger's voice boomed like cannon fire. Albert jumped again, hurrying to the desk next to his fellow students.

"There'll be no daydreaming on my watch!" Tightening his ponytail, Klinger stepped toward Albert's desk. "Do you know what happens to soldiers who daydream, boy?"

Albert didn't really want to know.

"They get blown to bits, that's what!" Klinger tossed his hands into the air. "Or worse, they get the soldier behind them blown to bits! Just look at this!"

The whole of Albert's desk shook as the principal's black boot came crashing down on top of it. Klinger grabbed the pea-green hem of his pant leg and jerked it up over his knee, revealing a grotesque scattering of thick, pink scars.

"Shrapnel in the shin," he crowed. "Grisly sight. Bone and skin — all over my uniform! Tibia showed clean through. Lots of blood, too."

Albert felt sick.

"And all because the rookie in front of me was too busy thinking about his family back home... instead of watching for land mines like he was supposed to!" Klinger grabbed a pencil from inside the desk and snapped it over his knee. "War is brutal, cadets! But not nearly as bad as the detention barracks. And do you know what your detention's going to consist of today?"

Principal Klinger didn't wait for a response. With his pant leg still above his knee, he ran to the front of the room and threw back the black curtain.

"Chalk dust," he bellowed. "Chalk dust! Chalk dust! Chalk dust!"

Albert's eyes widened with fear. Miss Maple screamed and the marker-sniffer fainted to the floor. Behind the curtain materialized a large room filled to capacity with used chalkboards; a catacomb[8] of corpses shrouded in the caustic[9] dusts of time.

"And all of them," Principal Klinger added with an evil gleam in his eye, "need a good cleaning. Now move, move, move!"

Albert looked at the red-haired kid on the floor beside them and wished he too could faint, only to wake up when the nightmare of cleaning chalkboards had passed. Because there was not a worse punishment in the whole world than the cleaning of chalkboards; nor was there anything more deadly.

As Albert marched to the front of the room to grab a cleaning rag from his principal's hand, he reflected back on a story told to him during his last recess. How Principal Klinger once got so mad he made a kid clean chalkboards all day long — with no food or drink or break or anything — until finally the kid had to go to the hospital where a specialized team of international doctors removed his appendix just in the nick of time. And then there was the kid who had to have his tonsils taken out because of all the dust he breathed in during his detention.

"What are you waiting for, Albert?" The Colonel extended his hand toward a particularly dusty board at the front of the room. "Get to it!"

Albert covered his mouth with his sleeve and swiped the blackboard. A thick layer of white powder fell onto the chalk tray like snow over an open road. Principal Klinger placed a bucket at the end of the tray.

"Now, wipe it into the bucket."

Albert did. But not to Principal Klinger's liking.

"Be careful!" he commanded. "You're spilling. I didn't dodge bullets for you to waste. Now, pick those up."

Albert looked down at the floor. One, two, three, maybe four particles of dust speckled the green tile. It was nothing, he thought; nothing worth screaming about anyway. But arguing was the sure road to a longer detention and Albert liked his tonsils where they were, so he dabbed his rag over the few flecks of chalk dust and shook them into the bucket.

"That's better. As you were."

Albert bowed his head. "Yes, Colonel Principal Klinger, Sir!"

"Well said, cadet. Now, no more spilling, you hear? I need this dust. We can use it again." Principal Klinger's eyes sparkled like diamonds. A strange greed consumed his face. "For other *things*."

Other things? Albert wondered what other uses there were besides writing on chalkboards and punishing the innocent. Why, even if they cleaned every board in the room, he didn't imagine there was enough dust to make a full box of chalk.

It was then that Miss Maple bumped her chalkboard, which, in turn, bumped another and another and so on until a small opening formed and Albert could see all the way back to the very side wall which, up until now, had been completely hidden.

At first he saw only one bucket. It was tall and white, and had the words CHALK DUST and its Spanish translation, *POLVO DE LA TIZA*, scribbled across the front. But then Miss Maple bumped her board again and the hole through which Albert peered grew in size.

A thousand more buckets appeared, maybe two. Stacked clear to the ceiling, they looked like a dreadful army of soldiers in formation. They all bore the same terrible words. They were all filled to the brim with the same deadly dust.

6

PARTNERS GO

The walk home from detention had been long. Like one of Ms. Hogsteen's lessons, it seemed like it would never end. But now that it was over and Albert stood in front of his house, he wished it could have been longer. Oddly, he didn't want to go home.

Familiar premonitions and concerns from the night before and the early morning came back into his mind with full force. In his mind's eye, he saw his parents sitting at the dinner table, silently stirring their food; and his dad saying goodbye to him in the car again, too, asking him to be good and help out his mom. Albert shivered. Something *had* changed. Something *was* wrong.

He looked up at his house. He looked at the windows. There were no lights on. His mind wandered back to the other year when they had first moved into the house, when things were good…

"This is going to be our very own street of dreams, son," his dad promised as he pulled the moving truck into the driveway. "D'you know this area is called the Gateway to the Old West? The Old West! Like with cowboys and gunfights and saloons."

Albert looked at him with amazement. "Really?"

"Sure as shootin'. What do you think about that, huh, partner?"

Albert stepped onto the porch. He had said it was cool. He had made his hand into a pretend gun and fired off a round in celebration. Imagine, he had thought. Their very own street of dreams!

But that had been a lie, too.

Albert kicked the porch. Things were supposed to be better here. Things were supposed to be happy here. But they weren't. Dreams, he was learning, could just as easily be bad.

Albert reached for the door. His fingers hesitated at the door knob, but finally gripped it as tight as they could. It felt cold. He twisted it. The door opened.

"Hello? I'm h-home." In his voice was a noticeable quiver. "Mom? Dad? Are you here?"

There was no answer.

Albert set his backpack to the side of the door and wandered into the living room. Everything seemed as it should be. He looked at a picture on the end table; the one of him and his dad and his mom — taken but one year before. He smiled. He missed his old house. He missed the days when his dad didn't have to work so much.

"Dad. Where are you?"

Still no answer.

Like the muggy calm before a storm, uneasiness filled the air. Even the refrigerator sounded restless. Albert stepped into the kitchen and peeked in. A large plate of chocolate chip cookies caught his eye. He took a step back.

He loved cookies, chocolate chip ones most of all; and he knew the whole plate was for him, but he also knew that wasn't a good thing. Because he only ever got a whole plate all to himself when something bad had happened, or when something bad was about to happen.

Like the time he crashed on his bike and skinned both knees real bad. Or the time he didn't win the spelling bee. Then there was time he got real sick and missed a month of school. And the time his dog was going to be put to sleep because she was sick. And then there was the day after his grandpa died, and the day — Albert squeezed his eyes shut — the day his parents started having problems.

Suddenly, Albert knew what was wrong.

In a flash, he opened his eyes. He tore from the kitchen and raced back into the living room. And it was all he could do to keep from gasping in horror. Skewed by imagination, the room had changed. Before his very eyes, it turned violent and destructive, everything a dark reflection of the unbridled confusion and anger brewing deep down inside of him. Shards of his mom's favorite vase fanned wildly across the living room carpet like blood spattered across a pale face. The couches and the chairs lay on their sides, violated; brutally searched against their will. Deep gashes ran the length of the walls — wounds too severe to heal and too painful to forget. The family pictures were missing; their empty frames piled in the corner like limp bodies after some pointless mass execution. A bitter breeze roared through the shattered living room window, striking at Albert's face. Torn curtains flapped this way and that — mangled arms flailing about in madness, waiting and waiting, reaching and reaching, then falling silent.

Albert spun on his heels, his mind running wild as it latched onto the first idea offering any explanation to his pains and confusions. Someone had broken into his house! Someone had forced their way in and kidnapped his parents. Someone had taken them to a dark, secret basement and tied them up to a chair and withheld food and water and hurt them — bad. Or maybe, the thought occurred to him, maybe the kidnappers were still in the house; maybe they hadn't left yet.

Fear seized Albert's throat. On a mission, he stepped over to the hall closet and removed his baseball bat. He was going to search the whole house. He was going to find his parents. He was going to bring them back.

Albert began in the bathroom, but there was no one there. He looked in the closet and the washroom and the guest room, but they too were empty. Finally, his eyes fell upon a room at the end of the hallway. The door was slightly ajar. A dim light burned inside.

The den.

Albert's breathing turned shallow. His heart pounding with every step, he inched his way down the hallway until he was face to face with the den door. He tightened his hold on the bat.

There was no telling how many bad guys might be in his dad's office. But it didn't matter. He had to be ready to fight them all: one, three, fifty, one hundred; how ever many there were; whoever they were; whatever weapons they came at him with — knives, guns, chains, chalk dust…

Albert dried his hands over his jeans and took a deep breath. This was it. It was now or never. Now! Pushing off the wall, he jumped in front of the door and kicked it open.

Crash!

Flecks of paint and drywall exploded into the air. Albert leaped into the den like a lion after its prey. Hitting the carpet, he curled his body into a ball and rolled across the floor, skidding to a stop behind the safety of an empty office chair.

"Give me back my parents!" he screamed.

But there was no one in the den, either. In fact, other than the office furniture, there was nothing in the den at all.

Albert's hands fell to his side. From his knees, he surveyed the room that suddenly looked so strange to him. His dad's den, it — it was empty. There were no books, no computer, no maps, no file cabinet, no garbage can; no dad. The shelves had been completely gutted except for a couple of pen caps, an eraser, a broken pencil sharpener and — and a familiar silver picture frame, lying face down.

Albert jumped to his feet and flipped it over. But where a picture of he and his dad on a fishing trip had been, a thin sheet of corrugated cardboard was all that remained. Albert's chest filled with confusion and anger. He slammed the frame onto the desk, shattering the glass across the room.

This has gone too far, his thoughts screamed. Way too far! How dare those guys take that picture! How dare they!

Engrossed within a swarm of emotions, Albert rammed his shoulder into the side of the bookshelf. As it crashed to the floor, he swung wildly at the wall behind it, connecting, smashing it with his fist. It hurt — bad, but he swung again and again and again and again — until a sudden noise from upstairs put a momentary end to his tirade.

Albert bolted from the den and flew up the stairs, threatening the assailants with his fists and as many swear words as he could think of.

"You bring back that picture! You hear me? You give me back my parents!"

Albert reached the top of the stairs. A light was on in his parents' room. Like a stuck bull, he tucked his head against his chest and charged. He was going to bust through that door and he was going to bust through it good. There would be no mercy.

"You'll pay for this!" he screamed, his voice hoarse with emotion. "You'll be sorry."

Legs pumping, Albert ran faster and faster and faster, then through the door and — right into his mom's arms.

"I didn't know you were home," she sobbed apologetically. "I didn't hear you come in."

"Let me go!" he squealed, kicking and punching as if his life depended on it. "Let go of me! You took my dad! You — ! Give me back my dad! Give me back my mom and dad! Let go of me! Let — me — go!"

Albert wrestled long and hard, but it was no use. His mom wouldn't let go. She couldn't let go. And the more he resisted the tighter she held him until he couldn't breathe at all and he had to give in. He didn't want to, but he did, his fragile body overcome with exhaustion.

"It's okay," she consoled the only way she knew how. "*Shhh.* Son, it's okay." Like blankets of rain over windows, tears streamed down her cheeks, staining them black with make-up. "*Shhh. Shhh.*" Gently, she rocked him back and forth — like she used to — when he was just a little, fragile baby in her arms. "*Shhh.* It's okay. Son, it's going to be okay. *Shhh.*"

But there were no words of consolation that could patch the wound in Albert's heart. Like the silver picture frame, his heart broke into a thousand tiny pieces; and every time he breathed, he felt the biting sting from its shards. The muggy calm had passed. The storm was upon him. The storm was upon them all.

With Albert still in her arms, his mom collapsed to the floor, and together they cried for a very, very long time.

"Mo-om. Whe-re's Da-ad? Where — is — he?"

Albert could barely get the words out. His chest heaved in and out, wheezing hysterically between syllables, and everything sounded like gibberish, but his mom knew what he was trying to say. She understood.

And so she explained as delicately as she could about *their* "mutual decision" and how *they* just needed some time to "figure things out" and "make things work better" and, "Dad's going to be staying in our old place — it's still vacant" and, "It isn't anyone's fault, Albert. Not really. It's... it's complicated."

Carefully, she danced around the finer details she was afraid might hurt him. It was too late for that, though. Empty dresser drawers, hangers without suits or blue dress shirts or ties; there was pain enough. Albert's dad was gone, and he was gone for good.

But it wasn't good at all.

7

Cultured Diamonds

A shiny black car zipped down the freeway, heading north. Behind it a ways, a second black car followed, then a third, and finally a white delivery truck. Pushing the speed limit, they raced ahead, passing cars as if they were turtles on a log.

Hugging the shoulder, an old brown Bronco idled with its emergency blinkers flashing off and on. It *was* an emergency. Inside, a man in a plaid dress shirt of bitter blues sat with his head propped on the steering wheel. He was sobbing. His shoulders heaved under their heavy burden; a burden that, today, felt too heavy to bear alone.

Paying no attention to the man in real need, the black cars cut across two lanes of traffic and exited. BLUE DIAMOND COTTON, INC., the emerald exit sign read, and in a matter of minutes, they were there. A heavy iron gate opened to let the cars drive around back.

Inside, underground, hundreds of Mexican immigrants in blue smocks ran about like chickens without heads. There was not much time; and they knew if they did not finish the day's quota, they might very well lose their own heads.

And so their gloved hands worked feverishly, taking precise measurements of chalk dust here and mixing it in test tubes filled with special liquids there. Their minds raced, too. Calculations were performed. They double checked their math, then checked it again. They had to be right on or the diamonds would come out all wrong; the color would be off or the cut; or they'd be as brittle as glass.

"Five minutes!" a harsh voice snorted.

From the clock, the worker's turned their eyes to the the lazy, fat woman they called *Caballo del Río*; The River Horse; The Hippo.

"He'll be here in *cinco* minutes!" she shouted again, sitting down to rest her tired feet. Silver steam puffed from her flared nostrils. "Now, move! Or one of you will find yourselves *unemployed*."

Unemployment. It was a terrible word that was not what it seemed. Any time something didn't go according to the big boss' plan, there had to be a punishment; somebody had to take the blame. And someone always did.

It was up to Al Godón to decide who that someone would be; and whether they were involved or not, his decision was final. But they weren't given a pink slip or a notice to empty their desks before lunch, nor were they deported. Instead, they were taken out back and *fired*, or rather fired upon.

That's what losing your job meant. It was, in fact, a matter of life or death.

"Faster!"

The men and women were already working as fast as they could. A man ran over to a large high-tech pressurizing machine in the center of the room. He opened the door like it was an oven and slid in an enormous muffin tin of sorts. Settling within each diamond-shaped cup was a milky white liquid; perhaps too heavy on the chalk dust. He set the timer then ran back to his station to clear his desk. After a few minutes, the timer dinged.

"*Uno* minute!"

He ran back to the oven-like machine and threw open the door. Plumes of smoke billowed into the air. A heavy-duty fan on the ceiling started up with a roar and the smoke cleared. From inside the oven, a tray of diamonds sparkled; perfectly shaped blue diamonds; the most rare of all diamonds on Earth.

The man removed the tray. Ms. Hogsteen snorted as much of an approval as she would give.

"Those better be good," she warned. "Or it's your job."

On the heels of her warning, the outside door swung open and in walked Al Godón.

"Time!"

Everyone stopped what they were doing and dropped their hands to their sides. Sweat beaded up across the foreheads of those with dirty work stations; smiles across the faces of those with clean ones. But then, from across the room, a middle-aged man's smile faded.

His chair! He had forgotten to push in his chair — again!

Stroking the tuft of cotton on his lapel, Al Godón stepped across the white-tiled floor and stopped just short of the man's station. He looked at the chair and shook his finger back and forth.

"José."

On cue, Ms. Hogsteen wobbled over to a large chalkboard. She grabbed a piece of chalk from someone's station and placed a second check mark beside his name.

José's heart sunk. It was one thing to have your name on the board, but to have *two* check marks by it; why, the only thing worse than that was three. No one had ever received three checkmarks, though. Your name on the board plus two warnings was usually enough to straighten any crooked behavior.

"Attention!" a sudden and loud voice boomed from the parking lot.

The outside door slammed open again and in marched a man familiar to all of the workers. Out of duty, but more out of fear, they stood erect and offered a respectful salute.

Colonel Charlie Klinger clicked his heels. "As you were." He turned to Al Godón. "Permission to take more chalkboards, sir?"

Permission was granted. Several workers stepped over to a series of doors marked *Pizarras* and began wheeling out a hundred or so chalkboards covered in dust. They were so dusty, in fact, that one of the workers, forgetting to put on her dust mask, fell to the floor wheezing and had to be taken to the company nurse's office.

The Colonel Principal stepped beside Al Godón and watched the procession until it filled to capacity the large truck idling outside. Klinger gave the signal and the truck drove off. In its place, two black cars pulled up.

"I also brought more chalk dust," Klinger reported with pride. "Detentions are up."

Pleased, Al Godón watched as the car doors opened and out stepped the members of his team, each of them hefting a white bucket filled with chalk dust.

But unlike Colonel Klinger, these faces were strange to the workers' eyes.

A large fellow with enormous cheeks and a black derby set down his bucket of dust. He grabbed a golden medallion of some kind from around his chubby neck and blew into it. Like a blowfish, his cheeks puffed to twice their size.

From behind him, stepped a man who looked much like The Colonel; tall and thin with silver hair. But instead of army fatigues, he wore a tan suit complete with snake-skin boots, a white cattleman's hat, and a loopy bow-tie. He tapped a silver-handled cane across the floor as he entered the room and dropped his bucket to the floor.

A giant oaf stepped up to his side and dropped two buckets of dust. His moustache dangled from his lips like two red peppers. His hair and sideburns were like fire; the scowl on his face was no different. He gurgled a loogie in the back of his throat and let it fly. It sailed through the air and hit its target, a worker smirking in the corner.

If his draw was as accurate as his spit, no one stood a chance.

Lastly, behind them all and without a bucket, a woman with long, flowing, dark hair sashayed into the room. She didn't say or do anything; she didn't have to. No one could take their eyes off of her. She was —

"Bella."

The woman glanced at the man standing by the oven with a tray of diamonds and smiled. He didn't mean to say it. It just slipped out. He offered a quick apology, but it wasn't necessary — because he was right. Every man in the room was thinking it. She *was* beautiful. It took but one look into her eyes and they were hers; they would do her bidding.

She smiled again, casting a wink at the man who could not control his tongue. His cheeks turned the color of a rose; his heart felt like it might beat through his chest; his hands turned clammy; his knees buckled; and then he fainted.

As he toppled forward, the tray in his hands flew into the air. All eyes turned to their fallen comrade, watching in horror, as his tray completed its arc and sailed down to the floor below.

Crash!

One by one the diamonds exploded on contact, sending bits of blue glass scattering across the room. Al Godón's face soured. His eyes narrowed in on the remnants of what should have been a good tray of diamonds; on a whole day's work — now a waste!

"Who's going to tell the mayor?" he erupted without waiting for explanation. His upper lip twitched with anger. "Who wants to tell him we lost his *dinero*? Or who wants to tell the Chinese we lost *their* diamonds?" The scar across his cheek darkened to a morose purple. "Or Israel that we don't have enough to buy up the army of Palestine? Who wants to call up Japan? Or Germany? Huh? ¿*Quién*? Who?"

Godón's chest heaved in and out. He had had enough. Someone was going to pay. Right now! He spun on his heels toward the man who had fainted. He was coming to. His eyelids fluttered. Rubbing the bump on the back of his head, he propped himself up onto his elbows. At first, he was unsure of his whereabouts, but then, in the reflection of the shiny loafers in front of him, he saw a sea of blue glass and he remembered. Like a kick to the ribs, the grim reality of his situation stole away his breath. He looked up at Al Godón, pleading for a second chance, but the look in Godón's eyes was beyond clemency.

The man thought of his family back in Mexico; his wife; his little children; his dog. He wasn't ready to die. Who would support them? Who would raise his sons? Who would pay for his daughter's quinceañera? The answer was clear. No one. It would be months before they even knew he was gone. Silently, he bowed his head and waited for Mr. Godón to call his name.

But to his and everyone's complete surprise, there was another name on the lips of the scar-faced mob boss.

"*Señora* Hogsteen!"

The fat teacher gasped. All color drained from her ample cheeks.

"Why? You can't do this to me," she rebutted, backing away from her station. "This isn't fair. I'm your — your *amiga*. We're on the same team. I didn't do anything!"

"*Correcto*. You didn't do anything at all," Godón shouted back. "You never do anything. And that is why you have to *go*."

She shook her head in denial, but Al Godón nodded his. His decision had been made. It could not be reversed. There was only one thing left for her to do. Run.

With her fat forearm, Ms. Hogsteen shoved Al Godón out of the way and took off toward the door, picking up steam with every step. The floor shook like an earthquake. The workers ducked under their desks and screamed. But Al Godón, ever the leader, remained calm. Without a word, he pointed at the man with the red sideburns, motioning for him to stop the fleeing sixth-grade teacher.

Sideburns grinned from ear to ear. He lived to do the dirty work. In fact, if a day went by without a chance to hurt or murder, he'd get all depressed — like maybe he wasn't on top of his game the way he should be. And as it was, it had already been two whole days since his last murder; the last one, of course, being, as Sideburns put it, "that pompous New Yorkian lawyer", Thaddeus P. Zookenowski — "all full of his foolish ideals and legal jargons and what. The least he coulda done was fight back."

Sideburns watched Ms. Hogsteen's fat jiggle as she charged for the door like a wild rhinoceros. He had never fought a former wrestling champion before. This, he anticipated, was going to be a true test of his abilities.

With a swift crack of his neck, he gauged the distance from here to there and leapt into the air. Flying across the room, he grabbed Ms. Hogsteen by the neck and threw her to the floor like he was roping a calf. "I's gotchya now," he hollered.

But Ms. Hogsteen, *The Hungry Hippo* of the W.W.A., had never been known to relinquish a title belt without a proper fight. And so she jumped to her feet with Sideburns on her back and roared the most terrible roar any one in the room had ever heard — part elephant, part lion, part banshee.

"Arrrggghhhaaahhhhh!"

Strings of saliva stretched from the top of her mouth to the bottom. She gnashed her teeth. She pawed the air. She stomped the ground and bucked her shoulders, nearly tossing Sideburns into a wall. But somehow he managed to hang on. And with a bulldogged grip on her triple chin, he rode out the bucks that followed.

"I's a ain't lettin' go you 'ol hag. Give up already."

Ms. Hogsteen not-so-politely declined. Sneakers squawking, she ran as fast as she could and threw her body — back first — into the wall. Then she flopped into a work station and rolled across the floor.

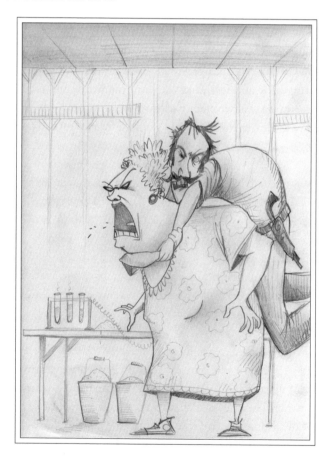

But Sideburns still could not be shaken. With both arms, he applied a python-like hold as he twisted this way and that — a move he had seen on TV some time ago. Ms. Hogsteen immediately recognized it; it was her signature move.

She looked at Sideburns and smiled. "That's my move!" she chortled[10]. "And I'm the only one who knows the way out."

Sideburns' face turned as white as a ghost. But before she had the chance to display her proficiency at the *Super Deadly Death Grip of Power Escape Route*, Al Godón brought a handful of chalk dust to her face and exhaled. Like desert sand, the tiny particles flew up her nose and into her mouth.

Sideburns quickly dismounted as all eyes focused in on the *Caballo del Rio*. She jumped to her feet and grabbed her throat, teetering back and forth like a tree in the wind. She took one step forward then two steps backwards and wavered some more. Her eyes rolled to the back of her head. Her face turned purple. And…

"Tim-ber!"

Hogsteen's body crashed to the floor. As a giant breath escaped through her mouth and nostrils, her chest relaxed. The man with the loopy bow tie stepped forward, jabbing at her gullet with the tip of his silver cane.

"Is she dead?"

Al Godón shook his head. He had grabbed the first pile of dust he saw — only half a test tube full. And with a body the size of a whale, she would have needed at least six tubes full to do the job properly.

"We'll take her to the usual place," he declared. "She'll have plenty of room…and *company* down there. But not you," he added, pointing to Charlie Klinger. "Professionally, you're too close to her. The *policía* will hound you. Find someone else to get rid of her. Someone else who can take the fall should anything go wrong. We have to be careful now. All of us." He looked past

Klinger and into the eyes of the others, chastising them for their carelessness. "Sideburns, Big Cheeks, Wild Willy, Veronica. What happened this morning could ruin us." He extended his arms to include the entire underground operation. "All of *this* is in danger of being disclosed to the world. I'm afraid we'll have to put off all planned-purchases and buy-outs. *Todos*. The Koreans, the Russians, *Españoles*, all of them. And that means no one gets paid, either, until this little *problema* of ours is…taken care of."

"Permission to speak, sir," Klinger interrupted, objecting on behalf of his comrades, but more so his wages. "That's only *if* he really heard us, though. *If* he tells someone. And *if* that someone believes him."

That was true. But *if* there was one thing Al Godón had learned from his lazy days as the son of a poor Mexican farmer, it was never underestimate the power of the mind. It was capable of imagining then building vast empires like he had done. But it was also capable of un-building them.

All they had worked so hard to build: a corporation; a dynasty; an intricate network of allegiances and powers could be destroyed in one fell swoop by the elementary mind of a mere mortal and his credulous[11] desire for change.

"No," Al Godón disagreed. "He heard *them* all right. His *compañero*, too. And until we have them *both*, no one rests! *¿Está eso claro?*"

It was; as clear as blue diamonds.

"*Bueno*. Now get to work."

And with that, Al Godón exited the room, leaving in his wake a disgruntled but determined gang of criminals. As mob boss, his job was done. His pawns would take care of the rest: the kidnapping, the torturing, and, of course, the killing.

8

PARTNERS COME

Albert awoke with a start. He was still wearing his play clothes. His stomach growled with hunger and he looked around for something to eat, thinking maybe his mom had brought him a snack since he had retired to his room long before dinner and subsequently fallen asleep. But she hadn't. Instead, draped from one corner of his room to the other lay a delicate sheath of darkness cast in through the window from the world just outside; a strange and brutal world; a world Albert no longer desired to be a part of. He rubbed the sleep from his eyes and scooted to the edge of the bed, taking several minutes to gather his thoughts and feelings like someone would a scattering of tiny, fragile glass balls.

It had been a long day. Albert sighed. Too long.

Outside, the wind howled, echoing his sentiments; and the restless clouds shifted, swallowing the moon in one single gulp before spitting it back out again. With a peculiar, detached wonder, Albert watched the nighttime shadows sulk this way and that — across the floor then up the walls; their heads bowed, their arms folded; in step with the dirges[12] of the night.

"I hate you," he said with a sudden burst of anger. And almost immediately his eyes welled up with tears again. He dropped his head, forcing his fingers through his hair. He wasn't really sure who it was he hated so much. His mom, maybe. His dad. Maybe himself. He didn't know. Not really. But it felt good to say it. Kind of.

Albert lay back down on his bed and tried not to think about anything. But he couldn't help it. Deep down, he felt as if *everything* was his fault; that maybe if he had done things differently his parents would still be together, downstairs, sitting in front of the radio playing a game, laughing; happy together — just like they used to be.

What if I had done better in school, he thought. His mind raced back unrestrained. Or maybe if I hadn't talked back the other day this wouldn't have happened. What if I hadn't daydreamed after I told myself not to at recess? Or what if I had taken the garbage out last week, or finished my homework when Mom asked, or mowed the grass during the summer, or what if this or what if that and what if, what if, what if?

Albert burrowed his head under his pillow, trying again not to heed the *what if's*. But they were just too loud! He needed something to drown them out. And then, as if by coincidence, that something came.

Tap. Tap. Tap.

Albert shot up from his bed. What was that?

The tapping sounded again, but louder.

It was coming from outside. Something... or someone, he gulped, was knocking on his window. Albert froze. A final series of *what if's* flashed across his mind.

What if it was the kidnappers; the one's who had taken his dad? What if they had come back for his mom? What if they had come back for him?

Albert jumped from his bed and ran for the door. But then, in a whisper that sent happy shivers up and down his entire body, a familiar voice called his name from beyond the window.

"Albert."

Albert stopped — inches away from an easy escape. His face lit up like a Christmas tree. And a glimmer of hope sparkled in his eyes. Could it be, he wondered. Was it possible?

"Dad?"

The tapping on the window came anxiously rapping yet again. "Albert," the man outside shouted a second time, "you in there?"

Yes, he wanted to yell, I'm here! But he was too excited to find the words. Fueled by a sudden burst of energy, he flew to the window.

"Dad! Dad! Da — !"

"Dad-gummit," the voice outside cursed strangely. "Maybe I got the wrong house, after all. Gosh darn wind. Boy howdy, this is some pickle."

Albert stopped again — this time just short of opening the window. A pickle? Like a child during winter's first snow, he pushed his face to the glass and looked outside. A fit of giddy laughter shook his belly.

It wasn't a kidnapper at all. Or his dad. It was even better! Better than he could have ever dreamed of. Better than he could have ever imagined. It was *him*! It was actually him! Sure as shootin'. For sure, for sure. Right there, outside his window, hanging on to a branch from the tree by the side of the house, *a man*; a tall man, dressed in a red plaid shirt, leather chaps and boots, and — and a cowboy hat!

The man motioned for Albert to open the window, which he did, nearly flinging it from its hinges. An icy breeze filled the room, but Albert didn't feel a thing.

With one giant step, the man from outside entered the room. Seamlessly, he yanked the dusty cowboy hat from his head, ruffled the sand out of his hair, and took an awkward bow.

"Whoooee!" he howled. "PJ McDougal, at your service. It's a real pleasure to meetchya."

He extended a calloused hand in friendly greeting, but Albert found himself entirely unable to move. As still as a statue, he stared in awe at the man in front of him; tall and strong; his cowboy clothes caked in dirt; his dusty blonde hair like a dry mop on his head; his face tough but kind; and his eyes sparkling like the finest gemstones on earth.

PJ shivered, pointing behind him. "Sure is cold out there, huh? Boy howdy!" He shivered again, rubbing his hands together as if he were in front of a warm campfire. "Cold as heck itself, I say. Sure could go for a nice warm fire 'bout now. Maybe a pan of beans bubblin' on the side. *Ummm-mmm.*" He rubbed his tummy. "For sure, for sure."

Finally, Albert spoke.

"PJ" he whispered with an air of reverence. "Is it you? Is it...really you?"

PJ flashed a toothy grin. "You betchya," he declared, patting himself down. "In the flesh." He stroked his now-smooth chin. "Why, who'dya expect? Santa Claus? With all due respect now, I don't think he'd fit into these here leather chaps of mine."

Albert shook with laughter. "But you're —." He paused. "You're real."

"Well, course I'm real." PJ slapped his thigh. "Heck, I'm as real as they come. You can bet your saddle on that. And your spurs, too," he added, clinking his together. "Sure as shootin'. For sure, for sure. Ol' Buck out there, he's real, too. Named him so on account of the fact he bucks so much."

Albert looked out the window again. Tied to the base of the tree was a beautiful brown bronco. It was almost too much. Why, he had just been daydreaming about P.J. and his horse earlier! He had let his mind wander and drawn them in his text book at school. And now, here they were — at his house — in his very own room.

"Sure is a nice room, too," PJ praised. He scooped his hair back with his large hand and secured his wrangled hat over his head. "Mind if I take a gander?"

Albert didn't mind at all.

"Yes, sir. Very nice room, indeed," PJ repeated, admiring the posters and drawings on the wall. "Is this one here me?"

He pointed to a crude drawing of a cowboy tacked over the head of Albert's bed. Albert blushed, but nodded positively. The wall was covered with drawings of PJ, his horse, and their many adventures together.

"Good likeness. Looks just like me. I like it."

"Thanks," Albert blushed again, pausing to suppress a childish giggle, "PJ." It tickled him to say his name. So he said it again, to which PJ jammed his thumbs into his belt loops and smiled coyly in return.

"Any time, any time." Leaning over, he examined a photograph on Albert's nightstand. "Now who's this? It kinda looks like me, but…" He scratched his head. "I don't seem to remember gettin' my picture takin' lately. Not fishin' anyhow."

Albert's smile vanished. "That's my dad," he mumbled quietly. "From the summer time."

PJ cupped his hand to his ear and leaned in closer. "How's that?"

Albert looked away. "My dad," he said again. "It's my dad."

PJ wiped a hand across his mouth. "Your dad, huh?"

He walked over to Albert and forced him onto the edge of the bed. Albert folded under his hands like play-dough.

"Sure beats all, don't it?" PJ took a seat beside his friend. "By George, if it ain't the gosh-darndest pickle ever, I don't know what is. Just don't seem fair losin' him like that, does it now?"

Albert's shoulders wilted. In his heart, he knew there had been no kidnappers involved.

"Albert?" PJ placed an arm around him and squeezed. "I wantchya to listen to me and I wantchya to listen real close. There ain't no use beatin' yourself up over it, okay? Won't do you a spot of good. None at all. You hear me? Believe me. I've tried on all sorts of boots in my time. And I've been right here." He slapped the bed. "Right here where you is at plenty of times."

Albert looked up at PJ. "You have?"

"Sure as shootin'. Take the first pair of boots I ever owned, for instance. Only five years old and I lost 'em on the trail heading West."

Albert looked away. That wasn't the same.

"Then there was the time I lost my dog to a fight with a big ol' black bear."

Albert was listening now. He had lost a dog once, too.

"And then the dog I got to replace him ran away with a pack of wolves. My first horse took a bullet intended for me. My old man worked three jobs so I never saw him much. A hero of mine died outside a saloon and was barely remembered. And my wife —." PJ's voice cracked. "My wife," he tried again, his eyes suddenly moistened by the gentle memory of their last moments together. "The love of my life — I lost her to the influenza only two months after we were married."

PJ lifted his handkerchief to the corners of his eyes. So fresh in his mind was that day, in fact, that it seemed to him as if it were just this morning when he had last seen her and held her and told her everything would be okay — even though he knew it wouldn't be. PJ wiped his eyes again. "Excuse me. Got some desert sand or somethin' stuck in my eyes." He wiped his nose and cleared his throat. "So you see, Albert, I do know how you feel. In fact, I know exactly what you're goin' through. And it ain't no fun, I know that too. But you know what else I know?"

Albert didn't, but he wanted to — bad.

"I know it ain't forever. Rain comes and goes all the time. Why, look what happened to me just the other day. You remember when I was fallin' from the sky, pushed from that crop duster and all?"

Albert remembered.

"Well, the whole way down I kept thinkin' I was a gonner. But I wasn't, was I? No sir. A Gila monster, of all things, saved my life." He paused a moment out of respect for the dead. "Then, after I'd walked around forever with no end in sight, I began to think the desert was gonna be the end of the road for me. But it wasn't, either." PJ removed his boots and tipped them upside down. Yellow dirt poured out of them like time through an hourglass. "Dang desert sands," he swore. "Sure is rough country that California desert; what with the snakes and buzzards and the *desert crazies* and things. Any number of 'em could've done me in. But they din't, did they? All of a sudden I had a new hat back on my head to protect me from the sun, and a new horse to speed me along my journey." PJ looked deep into Albert's eyes. "You catch my meanin'?"

Albert shook his head dejectedly. As of late, there didn't seem to be much he felt he could understand, or much he really wanted to understand.

PJ regrouped his thoughts. "What I'm tryin' to say is that it wasn't as bad as I had thunk it to be. I just wasn't able to see the whole picture right up front, see? I din't know I was just a few small dunes away from civilization 'til I knew it. And I couldn't comprehend that I was on the very edge of vict'ry 'til I comprehended it. Albert, you and me, we've been stuck in some real sticky situations before. And lots of times it din't seem like there was any way out. But we got through 'em all. Together. Ain't that right?"

Albert sniffled. It was. He couldn't deny what he had dreamed up.

"Then that, by George, is what you've gotta remember, partner. There's always a way out. Always." PJ tapped Albert's forehead. "You just have to put your mind to it, see? Then let time do her thing."

Albert closed his eyes, letting the words of his partner sink deep — like water over dry soil. Time, he thought in a voice aged by its trials. Was the answer to all of his problems really to be found between the hands of the clock? Was it really as easy as that? The very enemy that had taken away his grandpa and his dog, and now his dad — was it possible it could also bring them back?

"You can bet your boots on it. Why, time's like a great big band-aid," PJ beamed, proud of his analogy. "They say it heals all wounds, you know? And I'm inclined to believe 'em. Sure as shootin', partner. All wounds. For sure, for sure."

9

FOR EVERYONE'S SAKE

As the sun poked its head over the hills, it yawned, sun beams peacefully stretching across the land and into Albert's window where he lay fast asleep — far away from the confusions and pains and losses of the night before. So far away, in fact, that he was not entirely sure who, during the night — if anyone — had really come and who had really gone. In one hand, he clutched the picture of him and his dad; in the other, a pencil drawing of PJ McDougal. Within his dreams, they were one and the same.

But as is the case with all dreams — both good and bad — there must, at some point, be an ending; a final moment that succumbs to the light of day whether the dreamer is ready or not. For Albert, that premature end to a very good dream came with a gentle tapping at his door followed by a soft rustling sound as the door opened, brushing up against the carpet.

Albert stirred. His mom entered the room on her tip-toes. Making her way to his bedside, she kissed him on the cheek and gently shook his shoulder.

"Albert," she whispered. "Rise and shine." She sat down on the edge of the bed and brushed the hair from his forehead.

"Time to get up. I let us sleep in a little longer this morning. But we need to get going now."

Albert opened his eyes, blinking until they were used to the light. For a moment, he found himself caught in a fog; the kind that upon waking blurs the lines between reality and dream, when the dreamer tries to determine what is real and what is not.

With hope beaming from his face, Albert slipped off his bed and ran to the window. His eyes glanced past the base of the tree, then to the far corner of the driveway where he thought *it* might be. But it wasn't. His smile dropped. The Bronco was gone — for real.

From behind him, he felt his mom's hand squeeze his shoulder, but he was in no mood to have anyone give any of his shoulders a squeeze; and so without the slightest acknowledgment of her being there, he turned and ran out of the room, trying to hold back the tears he had spent all night dreaming away.

When he saw his mom again, just a few short minutes later, she was dressed and ready for the day. Her contacts were in, her hair was done, and her make-up was covering anything and everything she did not want him or anyone else to see. She looked just like she always did. She looked like nothing had happened at all. She looked, Albert thought, like she didn't even care. And it made him mad.

"You have to go to work?"

"Yeah." Her voice sounded shaky. Swallowing hard, she spoke again, but this time more calm and controlled. "I know," she said, her voice trailing.

Albert bit his tongue. What did she know? She didn't know anything.

"We have to keep moving though, Albert. Me *and* you. All of us."

Albert closed his eyes and took in a deep breath. A tiny moan eased from his lips. It hurt to breathe — like someone was standing on top of his chest. So he decided against it. Taking in a much deeper breath this time, he proceeded to hold it for as long as he could, his mind struggling to understand how in the world *all* of them were supposed to move on together. It just didn't make sense. But even if it had, he didn't think he really had the strength for it, anyway. Albert's chest began to hurt again. Pain when breathing; pain when not. Was there no relief to be found? A burst of pent-up air exploded from his lungs, forcing his lips to release their prisoner. His head hurt. His heart was pounding; his eyes spinning. He felt...

"Mom?"

"Yes?"

"I — I don't want you to go to work today. I don't want to go to school. I feel...sick."

Albert's mom stepped over to his side and took him in her arms. This time he did not run away, though. With the back of her hand, she felt his forehead. To the touch, his skin felt fine, but deep down inside of his tiny heart she knew that he was not fine — because she wasn't fine, either. She felt anger and regret and confusion and sadness and a great many more things that Albert did not; and no matter how fast her heart pumped, it could not rid itself of the terrible sickness brewing inside.

More than anything she wanted to stay home too — like she used to; like some of the other moms did. And more than anything she also wanted to let Albert stay home. But if they stayed home today, she kept asking herself, would they ever have the strength to go back? When would they ever be *well* again? And how would they ever learn to forget the very causes of their ailment? No, she shook her head, it was too dangerous. They *had* to keep moving. For Albert's sake. For her sake. For his dad's. For the sake of *their* family.

"Albert," she whimpered. "I'm so sorry. I —." The time she had spent applying cover-up proved wasteful. Like ocean waves, it crashed with the dark lines from her mascara; a masterpiece of acrylics smeared by an unexpected thunderstorm. "It'll be okay," she said, brushing his hair back and kissing his head. "We'll be fine." She squeezed him as hard as she could.

"Mom," he choked. "You're squishing me."

She let go, laughing — a little, then wiped her eyes and hugged him again, but softer. "I'm sorry. I love you, son. Do you know that?"

Albert didn't say anything.

"You'll be okay," she sniffled. "I promise. It won't be that bad. It'll be good for you to go today. For me, too. We'll be fine. It'll just take some getting used to, that's all. You'll see."

But Albert couldn't see anything. His vision was blurred, his head still hurt, and no amount of anything, he decided, was going to make him change his mind.

10

Foul Play

"Here we go." Albert's mom fumbled with the keys as she eased them into the ignition and turned it over. The engine roared. "Drivers," she announced in a nasally voice, "start your engines."

Lots of times, Albert pretended to race his mom to school. But not today. He just wasn't in the mood. Instead, he turned to look out the window. As they backed down the driveway in silence, then picked up speed onto the main road, he watched the definite shapes of the trees and the people and the houses soften until the world as he knew it was nothing but a blur, completely and unavoidably unrecognizable.

Albert's mom tried to make small-talk. For the fourth or fifth time that morning, she asked how he was doing. Then she told him everything would be okay for the sixth or seventh time, and that it would take some work and some time, but in the end they could do it — "together." Finally, as if nothing had happened at all, she informed him that he would get to see his dad later that night.

"He's staying in our old place. Remember?"

Albert wasn't sure if she was asking him whether he remembered the old place, or whether he remembered his dad was staying there. Either way, like the scars across his knee from the time he wrecked his bike, he remembered them both.

"We thought it would be really important for you," his mom continued. "And all of us, really. And it's going to be fun, too." Her voice increased with an excitement both sudden and strange. "Spending the weekend together... playing and hanging out and doing manly stuff. I wish I could be there."

"Why can't you?"

Albert's mom bit down on her lip. Albert, too. He didn't need an answer. He already knew. *Together.* That word meant nothing to him now. Eating breakfast with his mom wasn't together. Back and forth during the summer time and holidays wasn't going to be together. And going to his dad's house for the weekend — alone — was definitely not together.

His mom tried to explain anew that they all just needed a little bit of time — that's all — and that his dad was looking forward to it and that in the end it might help them all feel better about things. But Albert had heard enough. Reaching over, he pushed a button, and the radio crackled to life. On the other end, an announcer cleared his throat before speaking, his whiny voice as if it were filled with helium.

Still no leads in the case of the missing New York lawyer. His brother and former partner, Bartholomew T. Zookenowski, says he will not rest until justice is served.

On Wall Street, the Dow Jones continues to fall, reaching its lowest point drop since early last year. Experts blame the continuing increase in interest rates.

Regardless of the trying economical times, Blue Diamond Cotton has yet again posted record earnings. Blue Diamond's HR department issued the following statement:

A woman's voice softly articulated the announcement.

I speak for everyone here when I say we are ecstatic. We attribute our success to the public's growing demand for comfortable cotton clothing. We express gratitude to our customers and employees worldwide. Thank you. And remember, 'Blue Diamond Cotton. The Elegance of Diamonds. The Comfort of Cotton.' We hope to see you there in our cotton comfort wear.

"We hope to see you there," Albert's mom spontaneously burst into song, "in our cotton *underwear!*"

But Albert did not laugh. For the first time, he didn't even smile.

"Well," she said, lowering her voice, "at least that news is good for Dad, huh? Maybe he'll finally get that raise."

As she rounded the corner, Elderwood Elementary, in all of its glorified dilapidation, came into view. Students everywhere were lining up in front of their classrooms. She pulled up to the curb and stopped, taking Albert in a half-embrace

"Have a great day, okay? Promise me you'll try. Please? I'm going to try, too."

But before Albert could promise anything the school bell rang.

"I hate this school!" he yelled as he jumped from the car, slamming the door. "I hate it!"

Albert's mom watched her son run away — further away from her, in fact, than he had ever been; his little legs carrying him and a world of burdens across the front lawn of the school until he was no longer in sight. She pinched the bridge of her nose to keep from crying again. But it was too hard.

The radio announcer paused. A brief series of whispers with a superior took place. Papers shuffled, microphones adjusted — the broadcast resumed.

This just in: The unidentified body of an overly large woman has been discovered at the bottom of the ocean floor just off of the Main Street pier. Local deep sea divers found the body during a routine dive early this morning. The woman's body was at first mistaken for that of a whale. Foul play is expected. There were several other bodies surrounding the woman's. Due to decomposition, however, they were beyond recognition. As of yet, crews have been unable to successfully remove the woman's corpse on account of her massive size. Police believe it to be the work of the elusive Al Godón and his ever-growing mob family. The victim's feet were encased in heavy blocks of cement. She was wearing a purple muu —

Albert's mom leaned forward and slapped the On/Off button. The grisly announcement and all it entailed came to an immediate end.

"Enough of that," she sniffled in disgust, shifting the car into drive. "I guess I'm not dead, right? So what do I have to be sorry about?"

With the cuffs of her sleeves, she dotted her eyes, wiping away any lingering doubts, then cast a quick glance over her shoulder and tapped the gas pedal with the tips of her toes. Quietly, the car coasted forward, coming to a natural stop in front of the stop sign, red with warning. And there she sat for several minutes, pondering the meaning behind the white-lettered word, which suddenly seemed so significant and profound. In the background, her left turn-signal clicked off and on in a pattern that was at once familiar and soothing, like music accompanying her every thought.

Was stopping really as simple as heeding the warning signs? How many stop signs then had there been? Had she stopped at all of them? Or had she simply treated them as yields? Painfully, she retraced her journey that morning — then beyond, counting the stop signs one by one, letting her mind recall the time she accidentally drove through one and got pulled over, but was let go with just a warning. If the officer hadn't been there, she reflected, she never would have known of her infraction.

'I'm sorry,' she had apologized at the time, her bottom lip quivering. 'I didn't see it. It was so dark and …'

Albert's mom closed her eyes. "And I wasn't paying attention," she said, finishing the sentence so fresh in her memory. "I'm sorry." She looked into her rearview mirror toward the corner around which her son had disappeared. "I'm sorry," she said again, turning the steering wheel as she pulled onto the main road.

But just as she was completing the turn, she saw something! Out of the corner of her eye, amidst the blur from her tears and the dust on her back window, she saw it, or rather, she saw *them* race across the reflection in her rearview mirror. It lasted but a very brief moment, a quick flash of color and energy and light, but the images became so clear in her mind it was as if they had been right in front of her; a magnificent horse, its shiny hide dulled by dust, skidding to a stop then bucking back, nearly throwing the roughrider from his saddle to the ground. The roughrider, she thought, he was tall and strong and oh how strangely familiar he looked.

She pressed on the brakes lightly then turned in her seat to get a better look, but when she did, to her disappointment, no one was there. No bronco. No man. Just an old, rusty bike rack with a few kids' bikes chained to the poles.

"Humph," she shrugged, half-chuckling to herself, wondering if she was not going crazy. "Must've been my imagination."

11

DOING HARD THINGS

As Albert burst around the corner and onto the playground, the faint reverberations[13] of the tardy bell evaporated from the air. While most teachers were just now opening the door to their students, his class was already inside. Albert stopped dead in his tracks. Panic set in. He was late — again!

If you were tardy you usually got your name on the board. But since he had been marked tardy the day before, his was already there — in big, bold letters for all the world to see. And even worse, his name had a check mark by it, too — on account of his early-morning scuffle with Ms. Hogsteen — which meant only one thing: for today's tardy he would receive a second check mark by his name and for the rest of the day the kids at recess were going to whisper his name and snicker and remind him over and over and over again about that one unfortunate kid; the one that their older brother or sister or friend once knew when they attended Elderwood; the one who once got three check marks by his name and was never seen again!

Albert picked up a rock and threw it back at the ground as hard as he could. It shattered into several pieces and each went skipping about into the grass where they belonged, but at only a quarter of the strength they once were.

"Why?" Albert fumed about his tardy.

Why did Ms. Hogsteen have to be on time every day? It's not like it made a difference to her. And why did she have to write names on the board and give out checkmarks as punishment? Was there no room for mistakes?

Albert stepped over to the swings and sat down. Since he was already late, he didn't see why he should be in any hurry to be yelled at and embarrassed and talked about in front of his classmates. In fact, the more he thought about it, he didn't see why he should even go to school at all — not today, not tomorrow, not the next day, not ever. Yes, he thought, the sure-fire way to avoid getting the second or third checkmark by his name was to run away. Then his mom would really be sorry. She'd be sorry for making him go to school. And she'd be sorry for trying to make him go to his dad's for the weekend, too.

Albert squeezed the swing's chains until his knuckles glowed white like they did when they were cold from the snow. And when he finally relaxed, it was as if he could still feel them within his grasp. Running up and down his palms were deep, purple indentations. They hurt...he hurt — all over. But he didn't care — not really. His mind was made up. He was going to run away for good.

But no sooner did Albert jump off the swings to carry out this seemingly simple plan than a familiar voice challenged his decision and the very reasons behind it.

"Ain't gonna work, partner."

Albert stopped.

"PJ?" He looked around, past the tether ball poles and the four square lines and the sandboxes, to the Big Toy where PJ crouched underneath the slide. He motioned for Albert to hurry on over. Albert did.

"PJ, what — what are you doing here? How'd you find me?"

"Followed your mom's car," PJ beamed, pointing to the side of the school yard where he had tied his bronco to the bicycle racks. Buck was grazing between a blue bike with a baseball card in its spokes and a pink one with matching tassels and basket. "Real horse power beats that bottled up stuff any day, I say. And that Buck there, why, shoot, he's as fast as lightnin'. For sure, for sure."

Albert smiled. PJ too. But they both knew this little visit of theirs wasn't really about Buck.

Albert looked down. His fingers began fidgeting with the wooden chips covering the play area. PJ placed his hand over Albert's. It felt rough to Albert. It reminded him of his dad's hand, although he didn't hold his dad's hand much — not anymore anyway. He was too big for that. But sometimes — now — he kind of wished he wasn't. And that he could. Again. Maybe just once.

A soft smile illuminated PJ's face. "You gotta go, y'know?"

Albert shrugged. Did he really? Why?

"'Cause cowboys just don't run away." PJ thumped his chest then leaned in and tapped Albert's. "'Specially not us heroic ones."

"But — but I don't know if I can."

There were a lot of things Albert didn't know if he could do anymore; things he hated. And how was he or anyone, for that matter, supposed to keep doing things they hated?

PJ gave Albert's hand a squeeze. "'Cause you love who you're doin' 'em for, partner."

Like dew over grass, the truthfulness of PJ's statement rested upon his own conscience. A scattering of misdeeds flashed across his memory. And in the split second it took him to take a breath between words, he promised himself he'd try to change things once and for all.

"And because," he added, "this ain't about hate, Albert. Heck no! And it ain't about whatchya want, either. Never was, never will be, I'm afraid. This," he pointed to Albert's heart, "is about whatchya *have* to do."

Albert didn't say anything. Deep down, he knew PJ was telling the truth; and within that same deep place, he also knew what it was he had to do. But why, he pleaded in silence, did everything have to be so hard?

"You, Albert, can do hard things."

Albert wiped his eyes. His dad used to say the exact same thing.

"Now, go on and get to class, partner. I reckon it won't be as bad as you think." PJ glanced across the yard to room number D-15. "Shoot!" he suddenly and rather excitedly hooted, gawking like a child. "How can it be with a teacher as doggone *pertty* as that?"

"What?" Albert swallowed hard to keep down his breakfast, so disgusting was the association with Ms. Hogsteen. Why, he'd seen prettier apes at the zoo.

"No, no," PJ objected. "Sure as shootin'. Just look at her. Blonde hair, blue eyes... Boy howdy!"

Blonde hair? Blue eyes? Albert poked his head out from under the Big Toy just in time to see someone closely matching PJ's description zip past his classroom window.

PJ was right. To his utter surprise, it wasn't Ms. Hogsteen at all. It was a stranger. It was...

"Gotta go." Without even a goodbye, Albert bolted across the playground to the classroom window through which he peered, nearly fainting with shock.

A substitute!

Forgetting how tardy he was, he pushed through the door and hung up his backpack. The classroom was bright and warm. And when a foreign but sweet voice called to him, he felt a happy tickle run the length of his spine.

"Good morning!" The substitute looked at her roll, scanning down to the one name as of yet unaccounted for. "You must be Albert." Her smile was like a ray of sunshine. "Welcome."

Welcome? Were they supposed to feel welcome at Elderwood Elementary? Strangely enough, he did. For the first time in a long time, he actually felt like he belonged.

"Good morning," he replied sheepishly, careful not to stare; because PJ had been right — she *was* pretty.

She was tall and thin with wavy blonde hair wrapped up in a mesmerizing swirl of shiny red, white, and blue ribbons. She wore a light yellow blouse the color of spring and a grey pleated skirt that went down to her knees. She had two small earrings that sparkled like shooting stars; and when she smiled, the earth stopped turning. Her face was like porcelain; her smile an embrace; and her eyes like fireflies against the darkness of night.

"Good morning," she said again, but this time to the entire class. A hint of red colored her cheeks. "My name," she continued, taking the time necessary to smile at each and every student, "is Miss Laura Lovely."

Albert thought it an amazing coincidence she and his mom shared the same first name.

"And I will be your teacher today," she smiled a third time, "*and* for the rest of the year."

For the rest of the — ? Instant shouts of joy shook the walls of the aged building. Like pots of boiling water, Albert and his classmates bubbled over with excitement and question after question after question.

"Why?"

"How come?"

"Where's Ms. Hogsteen?"

"Is she wrestling?"

"Did she break her back in a match?"

"Did she get fired?"

"Will she ever be back?"

And finally: "I hope not. I really, really, really hope not."

Miss Lovely laughed, quietly raising her hand to calm the burst of speculation. "One at a time," she said. "One at a time,"

Happily, the children stopped their chatter at once and gave Miss Lovely their undivided attention.

"I am afraid," she rehearsed solemnly, "I don't know any more than you. No one knows exactly where she is. She did not show up today and gave no notice of her absence. I just got the call to substitute this morning. So, I apologize, I am not entirely ready. Please forgive me."

The students shrugged their shoulders. How could they not forgive her? She had rescued them from certain doom. Tyranny had been slain; slavery abolished. The fiery inferno, itself, was on the freeze.

I will be your teacher today and for the rest of the year. Could there be a sweeter phrase in all the elementary world? Perhaps just one...

"Now put away your books." Miss Lovely's cordial tone saw immediate results. "Today will be somewhat different. I need a little more time to prepare. So instead of Math this morning we will be doing Arts and Crafts."

She laughed at the kids' reaction and their enthusiasm for the Creative Arts then gave hugs to each one of them as they raced up to the front of the room to offer her the apple or the snack-pack or the juice box from their lunch. It wasn't much, but it was all they had.

From his backpack, Albert grabbed a plastic baggie full of chocolate chip cookies and handed it to Miss Lovely. In return, she thanked him and gave his shoulder a gentle squeeze, which, in an instant, set his cheeks afire and melted his young heart like cold snow under a warm winter's sun. Suddenly, his burdens felt as light as a feather. Maybe, he allowed himself to think for a moment, just maybe things would be okay after all.

"Okay," Miss Lovely sang, "everyone take your seats now."

They did. And within seconds the sounds of cutting and pasting filled the room. Miss Lovely smiled again. With keen interest, she watched each student as they set to work. In their own unique way, they were creative geniuses; masters of a craft most adults had long since forgotten — herself included. For some, their talent was glitter. For others, it was colored pencils. For Albert, it was Origami.

With renewed resolve, he folded the final creases on a red paper crane. It was for his new teacher.

Miss Lovely brought a tissue to her eyes. "Allergies," she said to the class, but she knew it was a lie.

The wondrous scene of kids at play was too much for her heart to take. Looking at them made her think of her own son. He was about their age. In fact, he looked a lot like Albert. She wondered what her son was doing. She wished she was with him. She questioned her reasons for being away. And then, she experienced a flash of memory, which rushed to the forefront of her mind a few painful mistakes resulting in their separation. And she vowed, then and there, to make them right, so they could be together again.

12

THE GATEWAY

Miss Lovely sat at her desk, perusing the stack of newly-acquired lesson manuals. A pair of small reading glasses balanced on the tip of her nose, which, from time to time, she scrunched up in deep concentration.

Rather than start another crane, Albert sat back to watch her study, until, after making a quick phone call, she stood up to address her students.

"Class," she said as if she were waking them from a nap, "I'm sorry to interrupt. I promise you we'll have more time to finish your projects later, but right now we must go to the library. I was able to squeeze us in before recess for a little history project."

"History," everyone cheered. "We love History!" They couldn't believe what they were saying. But so it was. Today, they meant it. Albert, too. Today, it was his favorite subject in the whole world.

"Good," Miss Lovely squealed. "I love it, too. Now, when we get there, I want you to find a book about a historical figure and write a paragraph about them. We will begin sharing our research with the class after lunch. Any questions?"

There were none.

"Wonderful. Shall we, then? Everyone single file. And remember..." She raised a finger to her soft lips and lowered her voice. "Use your *quiet* voices."

A colorful poster hanging over the door welcomed them to the library.

> Gateway to Knowledge & Imagination.
> Unlock the Door Here,
> Unlock the Door Anywhere.

Miss Lovely checked her class in before stepping out for a moment "to go powder her nose." Albert watched his classmates as they ran to the various sections of the library. They seemed to know exactly who they wanted to write their paper on, when that person existed, and where they could find the appropriate book.

Within minutes, their pencils were busy at work, furiously scribbling down their ideas. With a heavy sigh, Albert sat down to give the assignment some much needed thought. He wanted to do something exciting, that much he knew; something everyone would talk about; something Miss Lovely would praise him for and maybe read parts of to the class. But nothing was coming to his mind. It was as blank as a chalkboard during summer vacation.

Miss Lovely stepped out from behind a series of bookshelves. She saw Albert, alone at the table, looking flustered. Her sympathetic eyes darted back and forth across the room as if to make sure the coast was clear. It was. Her students were busy reading and writing, and the aged librarian, Ms. Pistol, was taking her traditional nine to five nap. Miss Lovely smiled. She could afford as much time as she needed with him.

"Hey...Albert?"

Albert turned in his chair. Against the drab light in the library, Miss Lovely glowed like an angel. Her face radiated caring and kindness and everything good.

"How's it going over here? Can I see what you're working on?"

Albert tried to hide the red in his cheeks, but it was no use. He turned out his empty hands.

"I'm sorry, Miss Lovely. I just can't —. I'm still trying to think of something to do it on."

If Miss Lovely were Ms. Hogsteen, she'd have sent him back to class with no recess. But she wasn't. And to his surprise, she wasn't concerned or disappointed or anything, either. In fact, she seemed really happy about the whole thing; relieved, even.

"That's great!" she shouted, forgetting her quiet voice.

Behind the checkout counter, Ms. Pistol stirred.

"I mean," she clarified in a whisper, "don't worry. Really. Maybe I can help. Two heads, after all, are better than one. Do you like to read?"

Albert scratched his head. Before his mom went back to work, she used to take him to the public library every week. Once, he even read all of the books on the *This Summer Read For Fun* list.

> Who Says You Can't Go to the Beach?
>
> that year's slogan read.
>
> Walk on the Moon?
> Or Fly through the Air?
> Just Open a Book
> And Let Your IMAGINATION Take You There.

Albert had been *there* lots of times.

"Yeah," he finally replied with a smile of his own. "I guess I do."

"Me too!" Miss Lovely exploded with excitement again, disregarding all together the napping librarian. "And I bet you like to read adventure books. About the Old West maybe?"

Albert nodded.

"Then did you know that this very area is called *The Gateway to the Old West*?" She could see that he did. "I knew you would know that. You're too smart not to."

Albert turned beet-red, but for entirely different reasons than the time before.

"There's got to be an awful lot of history here just waiting for someone to explore it. I think a report on someone from our local area would be really neat. Don't you agree?"

How could he disagree? She was so full of energy and life and enthusiasm, it would have been near impossible to say no to her had he not liked the idea in the first place. But not only did he like it, he loved it!

"I know," he blurted out as if what he was about to say was his very own idea. "I'll do my report on someone from the Old West. On a real-life cowboy. From right here!"

Miss Lovely nearly jumped out of her shoes, squealing as if she had just won a board game. "That's a great idea, Albert! It'll be an *A* paper for sure. Let's see..." Her eyes raced past rows and rows of books toward one section in particular. "I think you'll find what you need right over there. I just came from that section myself."

Inspired by her enthusiasm, Albert sprang from his chair, not caring to look ahead to the prescribed destination. And so filled with excitement was he, it wasn't even until he was half way across the library that he remembered to shout back over his shoulder a "Thanks Miss Lovely!", which he immediately followed up with a hearty "Yeehaw!"; or rather a giddy "Yee-" but a not-so-lively "-haw."

Albert had reached his destination. He slammed on the brakes, skidding to a stop just inches away from the entrance of the final two rows of books. His eyes penetrated the ominous, black lettering on the blood-red sign at the heading of the section in question; a section hidden deep within the shadows of the large room; a section no elementary student dare go; a section so vile it had been banished to the library's most isolated corner years ago; a section so nefarious[14] there were rumors it had been built over an ancient cemetery: **REFERENCE.**

A quick and biting fear gripped Albert's throat, rendering him, for the moment, entirely unable to cry for help or make noise of any kind, length, or volume. He looked back at Miss Lovely, who encouraged him onward with a smile and a thumbs-up.

Did she not know that the gruesome ghosts of peoples-past haunted the reference section both by day and by night? A second thumbs-up verified that she, in fact, did not and, perhaps, was entirely incapable of comprehending such an evil truth as that, so innocent and full-of-life was she.

Albert bit at his bottom lip, trying to calm the vicious hesitancy jack-knifing around his insides like a shark in shallow waters. The last thing he wanted, though, was to look like a scaredy-cat in front of Miss Lovely. So, hands trembling, he took one step in, then another and another; and the further in he went, the darker it became until there could be no light at all.

Hundreds of books lay scattered across rickety shelving, covered in layers of dust like shriveled corpses encased within a mausoleum. Albert tried to swallow his fears, but it was no use. Surrounded by the carnage of good-men-long-gone, he began to feel as if the very flicker of life inside of him were being snuffed out. More concerned now with getting out of the dreaded reference section alive than searching for a good book on cowboys, he picked the very first book his eyes happened to fall upon.

It was big and thick and covered in dust, though considerably less so than the others. He didn't care. He reached for it, taking it between his pointer finger and thumb, then turned to leave. But no sooner had he hefted its weight in his hands than a repulsive, nauseating stink wafted up from its black canvas binding. It took all of his mental fortitude[15] to keep from throwing up, yet rather than drop it and choose another book, his curiosity forced this one over and he watched, as if he were a spectator of his own self, as his lips puckered then blew a layer of dust from the front cover. Like a fog, the likes from behind which a pirate ship might sail, a heavy, grey cloud rose into the air, revealing in its wake a title equally as sickening as the stink it had caused.

A History of Dead Dog Crick

Albert gasped. "Dead Dog Crick?" The title was almost too terrible to look at. But he forced himself to again, then again and again, each time blinking harder and harder just to make sure he wasn't seeing things. But it can't be, he thought. Dead Dog Crick wasn't really real. Was it?

"Sure as shootin'!" PJ's head poked out from behind one of the larger and dustier reference books. "It's as real as real can be. 'Tween you and me, though," he whispered behind the back of his hand, "I wish it was only pretend."

Before Albert could say anything, PJ's head disappeared back through the shelving and in a matter of seconds his whole self was standing by Albert's side.

"Howdy, partner."

A jovial slap across the shoulders sent Albert stumbling forward, though PJ was there to pick him back up again.

"Let's take a closer look at whatchya got there, huh?"

With his quick-draw reflexes, PJ yanked the book from Albert's hands and began flipping through its musty pages like he was searching for a recipe for cornbread and pinto bean pie. Menacing faces flipped past Albert's on-looking eyes like strangers in a crowded subway. PJ stopped on no page in particular and read the name from the top of the page.

"Ralph 'Big Cheeks' Malone."

The name was foreign to Albert, but the black and white picture was not. It was the man from his daydream; the man from the saloon with the black hair and derby and the golden trumpet mouthpiece.

"Big Cheeks?" Albert placed a hand over the photograph. "What — PJ, what's he doing here?" His eyes glanced over to the following page. "And him, too?"

Adjacent Big Cheeks was a photo of one Samuel 'Sideburns' Magraw. The name was again strange, but there was no forgetting the wild looks of a cold-blooded killer, eight feet tall and ugly as sin.

Albert looked at PJ, his heart pounding, his mind racing. "But I don't get it."

"What's there to get? They're real, too, Albert. The whole lot of 'em."

"Real?"

"For sure, for sure. Just like me."

PJ pinched himself and yelped just to show his partner it was true.

Albert grabbed the book back from PJ and turned the page again; this time to a picture of a woman with dark hair and a light complexion. Veronica Lux. She stared out of the book like a temptress, her hypnotic eyes transcending the very paper upon which they were printed. They were big and full of light and —

"Beautiful."

PJ covered his mouth and turned away, his face crimson with embarrassment and shame. Albert could tell something was wrong, but PJ dismissed it as "nothin'." Then, as if he thought Albert hadn't believed him the first time, he said it again.

"It's nothin'. Really. Nothin' I can do anything 'bout right now anyhow. Here." He reached over and flipped the page. "Here's the last of 'em. All real."

In the final photograph, the man with the white hat and the loopy bow tie sat in his saloon at the front of the bar. Resting across his lap was the silver-handled cane. In the background, Sideburns and Big Cheeks were engaged in a friendly game of cards while Veronica Lux stood to the side of them with her arms looped around two strange on-lookers: the first in a dark, pin-striped suit with a sprig of cotton in his lapel and a scar on his face, and the other decked head to toe in — army fatigues!

13

DON'T TRUST ANYONE

"Albert?" PJ waved his hand in front of Albert's eyes.

But Albert didn't move. He couldn't move. His breathing had all but stopped, too. His eyes remained fixed on the hardened mug of the man in the background of the photo, the face of a man that delighted in turning daydreams into nightmares, the face of Elderwood Elementary itself, the Colonel Principal.

"Albert? What is it? What's wrong, partner? You ain't worried 'bout ol' Wild Willy, are you?" PJ leaned over Albert's shoulder to get a better look at the picture of the stuffy Stetson-wearing saloon owner. "Ah shoot," he chuckled, slapping the air. "Why, he's just a nasty ol' rich man with a dog ugly cowboy hat. All bowtie and cufflinks, if you know what I mean?"

"No." Albert's voice quivered. "Not him." He raised a shaky finger to the picture of the man in the military get-up. "Him — that PJ — that's my principal! That's Principal Klinger!"

"What? Your — who? Principal? Kling — ?"

PJ's light-hearted expression dropped. ' — er', he meant to say, finishing the last syllable of the principal's name, but he just couldn't find the sound. Suddenly, without warning, his voice had died; and with it his bravado[16], too.

PJ's eyes shot to the top of the page, to the full name of this polished criminal from the underworld, William 'Wild Willy' Klinger, then down to the caption directly below the photograph. He loosened his handkerchief from his neck, blotting the sweat that formed across his brow as he read.

> William Klinger (Far Right; A.K.A. Wild Willy; of Dead Dog's Wild Willy's Motel & Saloon) and his twin brother, Charles Klinger (Far Left; A.K.A. Colonel Principal Klinger) are best known for killing their parents at the age of one (or so the rumor has it) and for their criminal ties to the elusive mob boss Al Godón (Left).

"Twin ... brothers?" The word tumbled out of Albert's mouth like the foulest of curse words. "It can't be." His head shook back and forth. "It's gotta be a mistake, PJ. A prank. That's it! Someone's playing a trick or something. They can't be brothers, PJ! They — they can't. Only one of them is real! PJ, only one of them is —."

"No!" The tone in PJ's voice was both strange and frightening. "How many times do I gotta say it? They're real, Albert. Real, real, real, real! Sure as shootin'. For sure, for sure! Why, as sure as you and I are real partners, they're real brothers."

Suddenly, PJ's face turned as white as a ghost. Oh no! If they were really brothers, he thought, then that meant...

Piece by piece, a horrific series of events he thought to have been once buried in his past crystallized into a current and legitimate threat of titanic proportions. The saloon; the secret basement; Veronica Lux and Wild Willy; Sideburns and Big Cheeks and Al Godón and now... Principal Klinger.

"Dangit!" PJ slapped the book from Albert's hands onto the floor. A stream of sweat ran down the bridge of his nose and into his eyes, stinging. They danced with panic and anger.

"Partner. You're in trouble."

Albert could see that PJ meant what he said, but...

"Trouble? What are you talking about? I haven't done anything wrong."

"I know, I know. It wasn't anything you done at all." He looked down at his hands, stained by the blood of his invisible crimes. "It — it was me."

"You?" Albert didn't understand. "PJ, what was you?"

"*It* was," he retorted. "All of it. I think I've gotten you into some real serious trouble here, partner. The pickle of all pickles!" He pointed at the book on the floor. "'Cause if they're brothers and — and Willy knows, then — then sure as shootin' Charlie's gotta know, too."

"PJ? What? What's he gotta know? I don't get it."

PJ backpedaled. "I don't know. I don't know." The lie was blatant and obvious. "It's ... it's complicated."

"Dangit, PJ!" Albert kicked the bookshelf, immediately sinking to the floor. He was tired of things being complicated. He wanted to know. He had to know. Now! "Please."

PJ dropped his head, searching for the proper words. "Okay," he finally said, his voice hoarse with regret. "I'll tell you."

But before he had the chance to say a single word, the soft voice of Miss Lovely interrupted his penance.

"Albert? Are you still back here?"

Albert scrambled to his feet. She was coming to check on him!

"Quick. PJ, you've gotta hide! She *can't* see you."

PJ ran to the opposite end of the aisle where there was a window about half way up the wall. Outside, Albert could see Buck chewing on a clump of weeds.

Wasting no time, PJ grabbed the window pane and lifted himself up and through. On the other side, he got to his knees and looked back inside. "She *can't* see you with that book, either, partner. It's not safe here anymore. If your principal is one of them, you could be in real danger. You've gotta get out of this school. We'll meet back at your house. I'll tell you everything then. I promise. But don't talk to anyone else until then. Not a soul! Don't trust anyone, Albert. Now go!" PJ mounted his trusty steed. "Go," he shouted again as he buried his spurs into its ribs. "Go!"

Albert watched as PJ and Buck zipped across the playground and up a steep hill on the opposite side. When they were but tiny dots on the horizon, he stepped away from the window to retrieve the black-canvas book. Through its cover, he could feel the demeaning eyes of Dead Dog's most infamous staring at him, daring him to underestimate their crimes and their powers; even their very existences.

Up until moments ago Albert would have never imagined they could be real, but now — now he had no idea. The troubles in his life seemed so unreal to him, a series of bad dreams from which he could not awake, that the idea that his unreal problems could be real, suddenly seemed frighteningly possible.

Even more frightening than these mobsters from another dimension, though, was the enigma[17] behind PJ's words: 'you're in trouble'; 'it was me'; 'if Willy knows, then Charlie does, too'; 'don't trust anyone!'

A thousand questions flooded Albert's mind, laying waste to the peaceful plains of his soul like rushing waters over a broken dam. What, he wondered, had PJ done? And why? And was there any way to make it better?

"Albert?" Miss Lovely stepped into the aisle just before his. "Are you back here? I want to talk to you."

Albert didn't know why really, but he wanted to talk to her too. Somehow, he trusted her already. In fact, he wanted her to see him and ask what was wrong. He wanted to show her the book and tell her *everything* so she could say that it would be okay and that she knew what to do and not to worry because the nightmare would soon be over and that things could and would be happy again. But Albert knew it was too dangerous. Out of concern, she might take the secret information he shared with her to the principal; and if she did that, he'd be a dead man, for sure.

"Albert?"

Miss Lovely's dainty shadow fell across the opening of his aisle. The moment of decision had arrived. With no more time to think, Albert tucked the book under his arm and did the one thing left on his mind: he ran. He ran past the picture books and the story time circle and the computers; past the water fountain and the *Read for Success* board and the checkout counter to the doors where he hoped to escape without notice. But no sooner did he touch their handle than the amber-colored lights of hidden sirens began flashing all around him and an awful beeping noise pierced his ears.

The blood rushed from Albert's face. He had forgotten to check out his book! In one motion, he skidded to a stop, turned around, and leaped back across the security strip. He hoped no one had noticed. But someone had.

A tiny old lady in a plaid skirt and yellowing shawl stepped out from behind the checkout counter. Her silver hair, wound tightly into a bun at the top of her head, reflected the sirens' auburn glow.

Albert's eyes widened with fear. He had awakened the librarian! His mind jumped back to a story a couple of sixth graders had told him about Ms. Pistol, her sweet persona, and… her criminal past.

It was all a scam, they said; her timid behaviors but a ploy. She was a cookie made out of poison. Underneath her crocheted shawl, she was a cold-blooded killer. And they *knew* this because one of their older brothers once had a friend who had a younger brother who once had a classmate who forgot to fill out the checkout card in the book he was borrowing. She got mad, they said, and yelled at him real good. But he yelled back. And faster than you could say Dewey Decimal, she yanked him into her office, slammed the door, closed the shades, turned out the lights, and — *Bang!* He was never seen again. Ms. Pistol denied all wrong-doing at the time, then she hid the gun, they said, in a velvet box behind the checkout counter... just in case she should ever need it again.

A wrinkly hand tapped Albert on the shoulder. He jumped.

"I'm sorry, my dear." Ms. Pistol's voice was soft and shaky. "You have to check the book out first. Library rules. Here now, let me see." With some effort, she took the book from under his reluctant arm. "Rather large book for a small boy. Shall we take a closer look?" She stretched a pair of wiry frames across the bridge of her nose and read the title. "A History... of... Dead Do —."

As if a switch had been flipped, Ms. Pistol's sweet disposition turned sour. Her eyes glowed red with diabolical inquisition, and her entire body began to shake.

"Oh dear." Briefly, she looked into Albert's eyes. "Oh dear," she said again, returning her gaze to the book's cover. "Oh dear. Oh dear."

Albert gripped the seams of his pants, barely able to watch as her trembling hands cracked open the book. In the reflection of her glasses, he saw the criminals' pictures fly by. She stopped on the photograph of Wild Willy. Her eyes shifted over to the image of Principal Klinger and the woman about his shoulders.

"Oh dear," she mumbled a fifth time, slamming the book shut. "This is no good. No good at all."

Albert wiped his palms across his shirt and extended his hand as if to take the book back. "Can I please have my book? It's... it's for a history project."

But Ms. Pistol didn't say a word. She just turned in circles as if she were lost, stammering oddities that only she could understand.

Albert raised his voice, thinking maybe she hadn't heard him the first time. "I need my book," he said. "It's for history."

"No!" Ms. Pistol barked out-of-the-blue. "You can't have it!"

Albert's face burned with anger. He wanted to yell at her too, but the story of the slain student kept him from opening his mouth.

"Shoo!" Ms. Pistol said, swatting the air like he was a bug. "Go find another book. This is a library. There are lots of them here."

"Ms. Pistol?" From across the room, Miss Lovely's redeeming voice came to Albert's aid. "Is there a problem?"

"Yes." The old woman spoke certainly. "Unfortunately, Laura, there is. You see, this is a reference book." She flashed the cover in front of Miss Lovely's eyes. "And he cannot check out a reference book. Library rule, I'm afraid." With a condescending smile, she patted Albert's head. "Students can only reserve time to look at them, you see? And as a matter of fact…" Ms. Pistol opened the book again, this time pointing to a small yellow card pasted on the inside cover. "Yes, as I remembered. Our very own Principal Klinger has reserved this particular book. Hmm. I was certain he had checked it out already, though." She looked at Laura over the top of her spectacles. "Strange. I will have to contact him right away to remind him it is here or," she paused for an extra breath, "I could lose my…job." And with that she stepped over to the front counter, picked up the phone, and dialed the school's main office. "Dear oh dear. Not sure how it got there. No, no. Not sure at all. Dewey would roll over in his grave if he knew."

Albert watched with horror as she removed a small velvet box from behind the counter and stole a peek inside. She turned to him and smiled. Her teeth were yellow from too much coffee, but her soul was as black as pitch. There was no mistaking her intentions. Inside that box was the gun; the same one she had used before; and now she was going to use it again — on him!

He had to get away.

"Yes, hello," Ms. Pistol spoke into the phone. "This is Margaret in the library. The Colonel, please. It's urgent." She raised a finger to the air as if to say, 'wait one minute, son', then turned her back on Albert so as to conduct the conversation which was to follow in private.

Now was Albert's chance. But just as he was about to make a break for it, Miss Lovely crouched down in front of him, blocking his path to the outside world.

"I'm terribly sorry," she whispered. "Really, I am. There are lots of other books, though. Shall we try to find a different one? Together?" She looked over to make sure Ms. Pistol wasn't listening. "Besides, I'd like to talk to you about something anyway. Something really important."

Under different circumstances, Albert would have jumped at the chance. But not today. Nothing, he sensed, could be as important as getting away from this library.

"I'm sorry, Miss Lovely," he said. Then he dashed behind the counter, ripped the book from the librarian's unsuspecting hands, and bolted through the doors.

Beep! Beep! Beep!

"Stop!" Ms. Pistol shouted.

Albert heard her phone crash to the floor, and the library doors open. He looked over his shoulder as he skidded around a corner. Ms. Pistol was running after him — and for an old lady, she was as fast as a bullet. Her hands were fumbling with something too; something rectangular and...and red. The velvet box!

"Stop!" she demanded again. "Stop or I'll shoot!"

14

THE LEGEND OF
JOEY KORNWALLACE

Albert knew of only one place where he would be safe: the boys' bathroom. Ms. Pistol wouldn't dare follow him in there — she'd be fired, for sure.

Albert slammed through the bathroom door and flew into the last of two stalls on the left. Fingers shaking, he turned the lock and sat down on the toilet to catch his breath. First recess wouldn't start for another fifteen minutes. He would wait until the bell rang, he decided, then slip away to meet PJ back home. He had to figure out what was going on and why. Because nothing made sense anymore and the harder he tried to understand everything, the more confusing it all became.

Ms. Hogsteen wrestling him in the middle of class for daydreaming; Klinger forcing him to collect the dust from chalk boards for *other things*; the book in the reference section with the incriminating photograph; PJ's mysterious revelation; Ms. Pistol chasing him with a gun... The list went on and on.

Albert's head hurt just thinking about it. As a means of relief, he turned his attention to the words and the sketches covering the stall door. Writing on the stalls was specifically prohibited at Elderwood, but everybody did it anyway — even Albert. It was their way of coping with the stresses of elementary life. And it was the one rule they could break and get away with.

Albert looked over to a drawing he had sketched of PJ during his very first trip to the bathroom at this school. It seemed like such a long time ago now.

"Tommy Bergawitz," he read from another message directly to the left of his drawing, "loves Katy Clayfish."

He had written that one, too. He remembered the day well. Tommy had been a sixth grader at the time and Katy was only in the third grade. It had caused quite the commotion. And for a brief moment — one recess at least, Albert was the most talked-about anonymous person in school.

Albert's eyes scanned down to the bottom of the stall door where a student's sloppy scrawl blotted the corner. He tilted his head to read the inscription.

Joey Kornwallace was here.

It was dated last year. In fact, it was dated the very day before he...disappeared.

Albert bowed his head as a sudden and solemn shiver made its way from the top of his head down to the tips of his toes. Unlike all the other stories the sixth graders told, this one was different. *He* had started it — not long after his family had moved. He was shy and lonely. Joey's story was *his* story...

Joey Kornwallace was new to the area and the fifth grade — just like Albert. And with the exception of Albert, he didn't have any *real* friends, either. So, to help him meet new people, his parents enrolled him in after-school Cub Scouts (he wore his blue Cub Scout shirt to school everyday). But sometimes there are things a boy has to do on his own; and for Joey Kornwallace, making friends was one of those things.

In the end, he rationalized there were really only two ways to make people like him. He could either give them his popcorn money or do something crazy enough to get their attention and earn their respect.

Joey decided on the latter. So when two sixth grade boys approached him with "a dare to beat all dares", he accepted. Before an all-school assembly, he chewed five whole pieces of grape bubble gum. The sugar rush was so intense, he reached a euphoria[18] only a very few of the most devoted and most addicted marker-sniffers have ever experienced. Still, he went ahead as planned, trying not to giggle as he secured a bathroom pass, snuck into the gym where the assembly was going to be held, and spit a purple wad of gum the size of a baseball smack dab in the center of Principal Klinger's chair. Leaving it to ooze and settle a bit, he snuck back to the playground and bided his time.

When the recess bell rang, the students put away their balls and jump ropes. The teachers took the lead toward the gym and the kids followed. And just like that the assembly was under way.

"Attention!"

Principal Klinger lowered a megaphone from his mouth and closed the gym doors behind him. With great pride, he watched as the students jumped to their feet and saluted their leader, stepping to the right or left until a path to the podium was clear.

"Very good," he approved as he made his way up front and took the stage. "A little slow. But nothing a good boot camp won't fix when you're of the proper age. At ease."

He waited for everyone to sit down criss-cross-applesauce (it was a rule — to save their knees) then took two steps back and sat down on his chair. He shifted uncomfortably for several minutes while, unbeknownst to him and most of the student body, the gum molded around the whole of his posterior. Finally, he settled in quite nicely. Joey tried not to laugh. He looked at the two sixth graders sitting across the room and exchanged thumbs-up.

Led by Principal Klinger's staff, the assembly consisted of a hodgepodge of traditional class cheers, commemorative choral numbers, the Elderwood Elementary school song, and, of course, the passing out of the *Special Achievement Awards* to all of the students who had gone above and beyond Elderwood's expectations during the previous month. Sadly, Joey was not among them. But he didn't care. Not really.

"And now," a teacher remarked after handing out the last award, "you kids get the special opportunity to hear from your beloved principal. So put on your listening ears. Colonel Principal Klinger, the time is yours."

With a swift salute, Principal Klinger planted his boots onto the floor and sprang from his chair to take the podium. But as he did so a loud *riiiiiiiip* exploded across the gym. Klinger's eyes bulged. Joey's, too.

Instead of just sticking to the principal's pants as anticipated, the wad of gum ripped them clean off. And there the mighty leader of Elderwood Elementary stood—in front of the entire school—exposed and humiliated; shirt tails hanging about his waist; black socks pulled taut to his knobby knees; and in the reflection of his shiny army boots, a camouflaged pair of cotton underwear.

A collective gasp ruptured from the mouths of everyone present. The women teachers blushed while the men teachers tightened their belts. But the students, neither embarrassed nor afraid, doubled over with laughter.

Principal Klinger's head twisted around as if possessed by an evil spirit. His eyes narrowed in on his favorite army pants and the wad of gum from which they dangled, then they shifted back to the student body, searching... Two aisles over, three rows back, seven kids in, *kneeling*, grabbing at the happy aches in his sides, a smidgeon[19] of purple gum in his mouth, and the silver lining of an empty package poking out from his pocket.

"You!" Principal Klinger boomed. "It was you!"

As if a breaker had blown, all laughter stopped. Absolute dread consumed Joey's expression. He glanced at the two sixth graders across the room, but they were not stupid enough to make eye contact this time. They turned their gaze to the far wall. And just like that Joey was alone — again.

He looked back at the stage. *Wait!* he wanted to yell. *I can explain everything!* But it was too late. There would be no time for an explanation of anything. Like a hawk with its talons ready, Klinger (still in his underwear) swooped down from the podium, yanked Joey's feet out from underneath him, and began dragging him across the dusty floor toward the mysterious side door — the **EMERGENCY EXIT** the students were never, ever supposed to use.

Joey arched his back like a trout before its neck's broken. "Help!" he screamed. "It hurts! It hurts!" A number of Cub Scout badges tore from his shirt. "No! My badges! Please. Help me! Anyone!"

His eyes searched for a rescuer, but no one knew what to do and, admittedly, they lacked the courage. Helpless, they watched as Joey kicked and screamed and clawed at anything he could to stay in the gym: backpacks, chairs, students, even teachers.

"Help! Please help me!"

But Colonel Klinger's anger was too great and his flight too swift. A chair leg slipped through Joey's sweaty fingers. Then a denim backpack burned his skin as it tore from his hand; every missed opportunity bringing him that much closer to certain doom. Because who knew what horror awaited him beyond *those* doors. He would be at The Colonel Principal's mercy then;

Partners Again

outside; in the real world; where no PTA or safety committee could intervene.

"Save me! Pleeeease!"

Albert couldn't bear to watch. But no sooner had he closed his eyes than a violent tug on the hem of his jeans forced him to open them again; and when he did, he was face to face with Joey Kornwallace. Like the flames of a wild fire, his innocent eyes were but flashes of confusion and anger and terror. And in their reflection, Albert saw himself.

Help me. Please. Help. Only you can help me. Please...

Albert had to try. Palms sweating, he dug his fingers into the gym floor and anchored himself down.

"Albert!" Principal Klinger shouted. "Let go!"

Albert refused, gripping the floor even tighter. He had to save *him*. Because partners don't leave partners behind, he reminded himself; and deep down he felt that, somehow, in some way, he and Joey were really connected; and that maybe one day they could be partners for real.

But Joey's hands were losing strength. His grip was slipping. He didn't know how much longer he could hang on. And then, just like that, he couldn't. His fingers fell, his arms hit the floor, and the rest became history: a trail burned in the dusty floor; a scattering of Cub Scout badges across the gym; a cry etched in Albert's memory; an image of Joey calling out for help one last time — his body writhing; his eyes pleading; his fingers reaching and reaching and reaching and —

Clang!

The gym's iron doors closed as fast as they had opened, swallowing Joey whole like a rattler would a helpless desert mouse. He had been the weakest of them all, the runt in a litter of hundreds. But now, in the wake of his absence, the remaining mice were no stronger. They cowered in the sandy den that was their gym, too afraid to say or do anything. Many of them were crying, even the bravest of the sixth graders, but no one could blame them. A fellow student, though quiet and strange, was now gone... for good.

Briiiiing.

Albert jumped, nearly falling from the toilet seat. He looked at his watch. While lost in retrospection[20], time had come and gone. Recess was just beginning. Now, he told himself, was his best and perhaps only chance to escape.

With book in hand, he burst out of the stall and raced for the door. He grabbed the door knob and began to turn it. But then he stopped. He heard something. He heard... footsteps... getting closer and closer and —. Someone was coming to use the bathroom!

"Miss Maple!" a voice just outside the door roared. "I didn't dodge bullets so you could run in the halls."

Albert's blood ran cold. Ms. Pistol couldn't go into the boys' bathroom to find him, but Principal Klinger could! Like lightning, Albert flew back into the stall, but as he did so the book slipped from his hands. He watched in horror as it toppled across the tile floor, skidding to a stop just inches from the doorway. He made a motion for it then stopped, locking himself inside the stall once again. It was too late!

The bathroom doorknob turned. The door swung open. Principal Klinger entered. And then, the lights clicked off.

15

AN ELEMENTARY STUDENT'S WORST NIGHTMARE

"Oops."
Principal Klinger reached for the light switch again and flipped it on. Above Albert's head, the fluorescent bulbs buzzed back to life, but there was no shaking the sick feeling that remained in the pit of his stomach.

Using the bathroom at the same time as your teacher was bad enough, but being locked inside with a principal suspected of killing his parents was a nightmare-come-true.

Through the crack between his stall and the next, Albert watched Principal Klinger as he stepped up to the mirror and lathered the front of his teeth with his long, slimy tongue.

A few feet behind him lay the book. Albert held his breath and crossed his fingers, hoping and hoping and hoping some more that by some small miracle The Colonel Principal would not see it. But he did. In the very bottom corner of the mirror, he saw its pitch-black reflection.

"What's this?" Klinger picked up the book and scanned the title. His eyes grew big and his head jackknifed. "Hello? Is someone in here?" He dropped down onto his hands and knees and looked under the stalls, but he saw nothing. "Hello?" he said again, this time with agitation[21] and force. "Show yourself, soldier. There's no escape for you now!"

Calm and calculated, he lowered his body onto his belly and slid forward like a commando moving into hostile territory; a foreign territory that suddenly formed in the back of Albert's mind as if he were really there.

He watched as a mosquito-infested mud oozed between Principal Klinger's fingers and a merciless sun beat down across his back. From overhanging branches, a poisonous snake plopped down beside the Colonel and struck at his boots, while the very stall Albert was in turned into a small congregation of crude, mud shanties concealed within the lush, tropical foliage[22] of the area.

Klinger touched his nose to the ground and sniffed his surroundings. He tilted his ear this way then that, listening for the faint breathing of an unseen enemy. His blood bubbled over with excitement. But then, so did his bladder.

"Aagh!" He jumped to his feet and ran for the stalls. "Some things never change."

Terrified, Albert watched as his principal stepped over to the stall he was in and toed the doorway with his black boots. Albert closed his eyes.

Please don't pick my stall, please don't pick my stall, please, oh please, oh please…

As if in answer to his plea, Klinger stepped back over to the first stall, slipped inside, and locked the door. Albert breathed a sigh of relief. But then a phone, tucked inside Principal Klinger's front pocket, rang and Albert bucked with surprise; the bathroom being the last place he expected to hear a phone ring. It rang again. This time, Klinger grabbed it. Like a switchblade, it opened.

"What do you want?"

"It's me," a man trumpeted back. His voice was deep and raspy. "Big Cheeks."

Albert gasped into his sleeve.

Principal Klinger grunted. "I'm on *business*, Ralph. What do you want?"

"The smoke has cleared," Big Cheeks reported cryptically[23]. "The coppers ate it up. Like a donut." He laughed. "Thought our story was legit and all. They've even identified her body now. Keep trying to figure out how many it must've taken to throw her fat self into the ocean."

"Three," Principal Klinger replied without emotion. "It took three."

Big Cheeks laughed again. "Looks like *The Hippo*'s wrestled her last, eh?"

The Hippo? Albert's mind raced back to the events of the morning and the unexplained absence of Ms. Hogsteen. He put two and two together. With the palm of his hand, he stifled[24] a scream. So that's why she wasn't at school. And that's why she wasn't ever coming back. She wasn't sick or on vacation or wrestling; she hadn't run away, either; she was — dead! *They* had killed her!

Albert grabbed at his stomach. He felt sick, really sick — as if something he had done was the very catalyst[25] behind her murder.

"Well, I'm glad it's done with," Principal Klinger admitted. "That fat cow's been a boil on my neck since she started here. Worst teacher in the world, no doubt. And she should know as well as anyone that failing to measure up to our high standards has always been grounds for *dismissal*."

Big Cheeks snickered a third time. "And how about the boy?" He paused. "Albert?"

Burning bile surged into Albert's throat. Big Cheeks knew his name! But... but how? And why?

"He's around," Klinger stated, pausing to tear off a sheet or two of toilet paper, "somewhere. I think Godón's right though. He did hear you guys discussing those secret plans. He knows about us. About everything. The old Pistol called me from the library right before you. Said he ran off with a book. *The* book. I just now got it back. I'm not sure how it ended up at the library again, though, but I have my ideas and believe you me someone's going to pay."

There was a long, drawn-out sigh on the other end of the phone. "This is what Al was afraid of, Charlie. That kid's as bold as he is stupid. If he tells someone about our little operation and they believe him, we'll be in real big trouble."

Albert pulled at his hair. Afraid of what? Tell someone what? What operation? He didn't know anything. I don't know anything, he wanted to scream. Get away from me! Leave me alone! I — don't — know — anything!

"Remember the Cubans," Big Cheeks continued. "We can't afford to pay everyone off with real diamonds. If one more country finds out we've been paying in fakes, the whole roof could cave in."

Fake Diamonds? Albert's mind flashed back to the scene at the dock where a nameless father had met an early demise, then to the few seconds of the tiny meeting PJ had overheard in the secret basement of Wild Willy's saloon. He remembered the bad guys talking about fake diamonds and things and about buying countries with them or something, but that was it. He hadn't really paid attention because he was just pretending; none of it was real; he had imagined it — all of it. Hadn't he?

"Something has to be done then, Ralph. And now. If we don't keep his imagination at bay he could destroy us."

There was a long pause. Albert could hear whispering on the other end of the line. Big Cheeks was talking to someone; a man with a thick Hispanic accent and a voice as soft as cotton. He couldn't make out what they were saying, but at the very intonations[26], the hairs on his arms stood up straight.

Finally, Big Cheeks came back to the phone. "*Expel* him."

What? Albert's entire body began to convulse.

"*Matele!*" the Hispanic man in the background reiterated. "Kill! Him!"

"You heard it," Big Cheeks finalized. "Straight from the boss man himself. Do it any way you want. Just do it."

"Fine. And McDougal? What about him?"

They knew PJ, too? Albert bit his lips to keep his teeth from chattering. A warm trickle of blood seeped from underneath his two front teeth.

Big Cheeks chuckled to himself. "McDougal's a baboon. We'll deal with him later. Right now just get rid of that dang kid, so we can start production up again and get paid. And don't forget, we convene tonight. In the secret basement."

There was a soft *click* and the line went silent. Klinger placed the phone back in his pocket, zipped up his pants, and flushed the toilet. His boots sounded like a series of explosions as they clunked out of the stall, across the bathroom, and through the door.

"Bobby!" he immediately shouted. "I saw you turn that corner! Halt soldier! I said haaaalt!"

As Principal Klinger ran after the offending-student, his voiced faded into the distance, but the command of this unseen dealer of death refused. *Kill him!* The very words ricocheted in the recesses of Albert's mind like bullets off of cement walls.

Albert slipped down off of the toilet seat, his body still quivering. His head was spinning now too and soon his legs began to wobble. The world around him rocked back and forth like a helpless dingy in the middle of an endless ocean. Dizzy, he tried to steady himself. But it was no use. His body tipped this way and that, spiraling out of control, turning around and around — once, twice, then three times.

Oh no! Three times!

Suddenly, a mysterious glow caught Albert's eye. As if by black magic, it lifted him out of the surf within his mind and placed him once again on the solid tile floor of the Elderwood Elementary school bathroom. His eyes shot across the way to the lone mirror, glowing red like a bloodshot eye. At its very center, a black and sordid pupil formed and in that pupil two images appeared: a man and a woman; their faces warped by pain and suffering and injustice; their lives taken from them prematurely by the scheming hands of family.

It was the principal's parents!

The rumor was true!

But Albert was not afraid. In fact, strangely, for a very brief moment, he actually felt comforted by their presence. Looking deep into their eyes, he saw a sadness and a love familiar to him — as if they knew what he was going through; as if they knew him and he knew them, too. No words were exchanged and yet, in the few seconds Albert had before he rushed out the door to find PJ, a conversation was had.

'Save us,' they seemed to say to him. 'Help us find the way. There is always a way.'

16

Real Danger

"They're going to kill me, PJ!"

PJ sat on the edge of the bed, gnawing his fingers raw as he listened to his partner detail the horrors that befell him while locked in the bathroom with The Colonel Principal. It was too much for PJ to stomach. And when Albert's story finally drew to a close, it was all either of them could do to keep from fainting, so overcome were they with fear and exhaustion.

For Albert, life as he knew it was in danger. It wasn't safe for him at home anymore. And as much as he hated to admit it, there was only one place he could go where no one would find him; only one place he would be safe: his dad's.

"I *have* to go." Albert's voice broke. "Tonight." He looked at the clock. "Now. I don't have any choice. My mom says I have to go… alone. And I don't think I can ever come back. Not until things change anyways."

PJ dropped to his knees, his expression plastered with hurt and abandonment. He was losing his partner — right before his very eyes — and it was all his fault. A wave of guilt swept over him like a landslide of mud and trees and rocks; and, for the first time in a long time, he began to cry.

As if by baptism, layers of filth washed away from his cheeks, revealing in their trenches a delicate skin very few, if any, had ever seen. He shook his head in disgust, slinging sand from his dusty mane like passengers from a sinking ship. He jumped from the bed and spun on his heels. His spurs dug deep into the carpet. His hands fused into tight balls, and he ran to the wall and slammed them into it. Then he brought back his boot and kicked it, too. Then again! And again! And again!

Made brittle by force, it gave way. A large chunk of drywall crumbled to the floor; and with it the beginnings of Albert's trust in PJ. As he stared into the wild eyes of his partner, a cowboy he once thought he knew, he felt fear. He had never seen him act like this before. Never. Something was wrong — really wrong.

"Gosh dangit!" PJ cussed, stomping the section of drywall into a powder as fine as chalk dust. "Gosh dang those eyes, those eyes, those eyes!"

Eyes? Albert looked away. He hesitated. Deep down he sensed that this was something he didn't really want to know about. Yet further down, he knew that it was something he had to know. He needed things to make sense. And so he pursued it.

"PJ? What eyes?"

PJ too looked away. A long pause followed wherein he dropped to his knees and tried with all his might to fix the hole in the wall. But it was no use.

"I'm sorry," he wept, pointing to the damage he had caused. "I'm sorry."

He took a deep breath, his mind reeling; and when he finally looked up from the floor, his scarlet eyelids were all but swollen shut; and when he spoke, a deep regret hung on his every word.

"I first wanted to tell you when we were under the Big Toy. Then in the library, I knew I had to tell you." He reached for

Albert, swallowing him up within his strong embrace. "But I wasn't real sure how and I kept hopin' it wasn't so and that maybe things hadn't happened the way I remembered them or that maybe I could change things, but...but I can't. I can't, Albert. What's done is done. I — I — I sold you out, partner. I'm a gosh dang traitor! Those bad guys know 'bout you 'cause of me."

Albert pulled away.

"I'm sorry," PJ sobbed again, falling to his knees. "Albert, I'm so sorry. I din't mean to. I swear on ol' Red's grave. But *they* saw me and they put me under some kinda spell er somethin' and made me tell 'em about you. So I told 'em. 'Cause I din't wanna die and leave you — not all of this." He pointed to the pictures on the wall depicting their many adventures together. "'Cause you're my partner. And partners don't leave partners behind, right?"

Albert didn't know anymore. It was supposed to be right. But partners didn't stab each other in the back, either.

"You've gotta understand, Albert. I din't think it would matter none. I din't think they'd really find you. But they did. They did. And now we're all in trouble. Dang that saloon! I shoulda never stayed *after*. Dang those eyes! Those *Celestial Saloon Girls* and the Klingers. Dang them all to — !"

"After?" Albert could barely bring himself to look at his partner. "After what?"

PJ wiped the snot from his nose with the corner of his handkerchief. "After," he said. "You know. After *you* left me."

Albert's head jerked back as if he had been punched in the nose. He didn't leave anyone. You're the one who left, he wanted to scream. You! I didn't do anything wrong. It was you!

PJ cleared his throat. "After you got in trouble for daydreamin' is what I mean."

"After I stopped?" Albert's brow crumpled with confusion. "But PJ, there was no *after*. I got in trouble. You just said it. I stopped daydreaming. I served detention. I cleaned chalkboards. That was it. That was *the end*."

Albert looked at his partner, pleading with him to say that for once he was right. But that was the one thing PJ, in truth, could not bring himself to say.

"Albert." An uncomfortable moment of silence followed. "There *was* an *after*. Sure as shootin'. For sure, for sure."

Albert's eyes closed, the grim reality of everything settling across his mind like dirt shoveled over a coffin.

"I kept on goin'," PJ finally began to explain. "I let curiosity get to me and I went down them saloon stairs even further. And that — that's when I really got a good look at *her*. And — and — and I couldn't pull away. 'Cause her eyes — her eyes, Albert, they were too…"

"Beautiful."

From within the shadowy sanctuary of the stairwell leading to the saloon's secret basement, PJ stared deep into the mesmerizing eyes of the woman sitting at the table next to the ugly man with the sideburns, the handsome one with the silver-handled cane, and the fat one with the black derby.

"Whooee. For sure, for sure."

Out of all his many adventures, he had never seen anyone as beautiful as she. Sure as shootin', he wasted no time in deciding, he *had* to meet her. And so he began his descent, unaware that more than just a whimsical[27] desire for romance was behind his rash decision to step into the light and meet this seemingly most celestial saloon girl. As if he were under the control of an unseen puppeteer, he made his way down the remaining steps, right into the middle of their secret meeting.

All eyes and one *Gentleman Six-shooter* turned to him. But PJ was the quicker draw.

Bang!

Sideburns dropped his gun and screamed. He looked at his shooting hand. The skin immediately surrounding the wound turned white with shock. He grabbed it and squeezed, then watched as the tardy blood began seeping through his fingers.

From across the room, PJ blew smoke from the tip of his gun and spun it back into his holster. Strangely unaffected by the fact he had just shot someone, he took a casual step closer, his eyes still fixed on the porcelain face of the woman in black. He felt empowered by her.

"Ma'am."

The woman returned his greeting with a wink. "Impressive."

But Sideburns was far from impressed. He kicked his chair into a corner and stumbled forward, drunk with anger.

"Why, you's dirty yella-bellied son of a coyote! I's a gonna kill you's! Like that dang New Yorkian stink-of-a-lawyer. I's a gonna tear you's apart!"

With his one good hand, he grabbed PJ by the neck and lifted him into the air, shaking him back and forth and from side to side. PJ's boots fell to the floor, his hat too; and had Sideburns been allowed to rattle him any longer, his arms and legs surely would have been next. But as it was, the man in the white hat and loopy bow tie had seen enough. The tip of his silver-handled cane came crashing down over the table.

"Enough. Put the stranger down."

"Put him what?" Sideburns' chest puffed in and out like a bellows. The fire inside him was hotter than Hell. "But he's just gone an' shot my's hand, Willy! No way in heck am I's gonna let this desert dog go without a proper beatin.'"

"Samuel 'Sideburns' Magraw!" the gentleman raised his voice. "I said put him down." From the inner suit pocket over his left breast, he withdrew a black pistol with a wooden handle and pointed it at Sideburns' other hand. "Do it. Just trust me, Sam. You'll have your day soon enough."

The red-haired oaf looked at Willy as if to say 'I's better', then blew at his moustache and lowered PJ down into a chair in the center of the room. "'Pologies," he said between his teeth. "Din't mean no harm."

"Certainly not," Willy concurred, stepping in front of PJ. "Our sincerest apologies, cowboy. Trust me when I say *Wild Willy's Motel and Saloon* welcomes all kinds here. It doesn't matter what your profession is or who your daddy *was*. Here in Dead Dog, we always turn a blind eye. What's an eavesdropper next to a murderer anyway, eh?" He brushed the wrinkles out of PJ's red shirt. "Now, to compensate you for the unauthorized beating you took, I'd like to offer you a drink. On the house, of course." Willy looked over his shoulder and snapped his fingers. "Miss Veronica Lux. Please bring this man a whiskey."

"Uh," PJ objected timidly. "Much obliged. But can you make that a Sarsaparilla? See, I kinda swore off the hard stuff after a real close friend of mine had too much to drink once and...uh...slipped on some manure and...uh...well, he died."

Willy nodded. With a smile, the woman at the table rose from her chair, removed a shot glass from a black, sequined garter under her dress, and poured a whiskey just the same.

PJ licked his lips, too preoccupied to notice the switch. With an uncharacteristic guilty pleasure, he watched as her body sashayed toward him like a snake slithering through the air.

"Howdy, cowboy."

Her voice, like venom, was subtle and warm and intoxicating; and it melted PJ's heart like butter over flame-broiled corn-on-the-cob. Without another word, she lifted the glass to his chapped lips and tipped the cool, brackish[28] liquid down. Then she forced him to drink another and another and another until he was like a baby with his first bottle, and more alcohol was dribbling down his chin than into his mouth. But he didn't care. A sheepish smile spread across his face; Veronica's too. Giggling like a school girl, she retrieved his hat and boots and proceeded to restore all of his cowboy dignity.

"There." She sat down on his lap and ran her fingers down his chest. "You don't want to lose those. After all, a cowboy without his hat and boots isn't really much of a cowboy at all." Her delicate hand floated back up to his face and began to play with the scruff on his chin. "Ouch," she suddenly pouted. "You need a shave."

"The d-desert air m-makes 'em gr-grow," PJ bumbled. "Norm'ly I c-clean up before I m-meet a wo-wo-wo —." He took a big breath. "A woman as *p-pertty* as you."

Veronica's eyelashes fluttered like a butterfly's wings. "Big Cheeks. Bring me a razor." She cast another wink in PJ's direction. "Then how about a shave on the house, too?"

PJ, again, was much obliged. A free shave was always appreciated, especially in the middle of nowhere from one of Wild Willy's most prized saloon girls. He tried to say thank you, but "beautiful" was the only word that came out.

Veronica batted her eyes again. Big Cheeks stepped from behind a curtain wheeling a silver cart atop which several items had been placed: a bowl filled with warm water, a comb, a pair of scissors, and a sharp straight-razor.

Veronica grabbed the razor. With one hand on PJ's cheek and the other across his forehead, she guided his head back against the chair. Her fingers coursed through his matted locks.

"Just relax," she whispered, "and look into my eyes."

Gladly, thought PJ, and with that he did her bidding. Pupil met pupil. But unbeknownst to PJ, there was more to her eyes than meets the eye. In them, through them, and by them, he became as lost as ever he'd been. The room about him began to spin. And then, in the blink of an eye, everything vanished — everything and everyone, that is, but the woman with the bewitching eyes.

"Good. Now, I want *you*," she teased, pausing to lather his face with shaving cream, "to help me. Can you do that?"

As if in a trance, PJ promised that he could and would. Veronica opened the razor and ran it down his cheek.

"Good," she said again. "First things first, then. You may call me Miss Lux. Or Veronica, if you like. But what shall I call you?"

Shoot, thought PJ, she could call him whatever she wanted to. "But," he said absentmindedly, "my real name's Patrick James. PJ's what my closest friends call me though. PJ McDougal."

She leaned forward to whisper in his ear. Her hair brushed his cheek. The sweet scent of her perfume nearly melted him to the floor. "PJ it is, then. It's a pleasure to meet you, cowboy."

PJ intended to say that it was a pleasure to meet her too, but this time "For sure, for sure" was all that came out.

Veronica smiled. She rinsed the cream from the razor and dried it on a towel. Seconds later, PJ felt the sting of the blade on the other side of his face.

"Oh. PJ, can I ask you one more question? Pretty please?"

"Shoot away."

Willy grabbed Sideburns' gun to keep him from doing just that.

"You didn't happen to maybe overhear what we were talking about just a little bit ago, did you?"

There was no hesitation in PJ's reply.

"You mean the part 'bout makin' fake diamonds and buyin' out other countries and working with Al Godón and things? Yes Ma'am. Every single word."

He hated to admit that he had been snooping around, but he couldn't lie — not to her, anyway.

Miss Lux cocked her head to the side. She washed the blade again then brought it to the front of his neck and scraped it down his jugular. The dirty stubbles fell like rain.

"And was there anyone else with you at that time?" She pressed her body against his. "A close *friend* perhaps?"

PJ's cheeks bloomed. He knew what she was getting at. "Shucks. You don't have to worry 'bout that now. I'm as single as can be. And I do my own cookin' and washin', too, so there ain't no reason it can't work out 'tween me and you just fine. For sure, for sure."

Veronica said she was glad to hear that. "But how about a partner, then?" Everyone knew cowboys traveled with partners. "Was your partner with you? Did he overhear anything, by chance?"

PJ shrugged his shoulders. "I reckon so. Can't say for sure. You'd have to ask him yourselves. I don't think he's ready for a shave like this, though."

Veronica glanced back at the others. They were all thinking the same thing. If this mystery partner was also privy[29] to their plans, then he had to be stopped before he got help — which meant killing PJ now wouldn't do them any good at all. No, they needed him to lead them to his partner. They needed to destroy the partnership together or not at all.

"And tell me PJ, who is this brave partner of yours?"

Veronica rubbed her cheek against PJ's now-smooth skin. With the tip of her nose, she traced the rugged outline of his jawbone down to his lips where, without provocation, hers met his.

Sweeter than a bottle of the finest Sarsaparilla, the kiss overflowed with power and passion. In an instant, PJ went from hazy to completely forgetting who he was, where he was, why, when and how. He pulled away for a breath of air then leaned in for more. But this time Veronica's fingers stopped his lips just shy of hers.

"His name," she pressed. "Tell me your partner's name."

PJ licked his lips. They were still sweet. "His name? Uh...sure, sure. His name is...uh...his name is...I mean his name is...uh..."

Man, he wanted that kiss back! He couldn't think straight without it. Why, he hadn't been kissed like that since...

PJ closed his eyes. Independent of his surroundings, his mind rolled back through time to a night he would never forget; to a beautiful home and a warmly lit porch upon which he stood, holding hands with the true love of his life. Bold and foolish, he recited for her the simple songs of his cowboy heart then took her in his arms and kissed her real good. To his surprise, she burst with excited laughter and kissed him back, but better, and the rest was history.

All at once, PJ's eyes shot open. In the dark recesses of his mind a light had clicked on. The spell inflicted by Veronica's gaze was broken.

"No!" PJ shouted, jumping from his chair. "I can't tell you. I won't betray my partner. You'll have to beat it outta me."

"My's pleasure," came Sideburns eager reply. Cracking his knuckles, he took one giant step forward. Big Cheeks and Wild Willy hovered behind him, eyes narrowed, fists clenched.

"Wait," PJ protested. "That was just an expression. How 'bout we talk this through? Like real men."

But Sideburns was not one for waiting or talking. Baring his rotten teeth, he zeroed his good fist in on PJ's face.

"This here's for my's hand," he growled.

Pow!

Bloody knuckles met malleable[30] nose and everything went black. The taste of blood filled PJ's mouth.

Pow!

Sideburns hit PJ again, this time sending his hat to the floor and his head spinning into oblivion[31].

Pow! Pow! Pow!

PJ's head snapped back again. Each blow felt like a jack hammer. His ears were ringing, his face was numb, and if he got hit again, he thought, it might very well take him out of this world. He scrambled to his feet, but only to be knocked down again by a slap across the chest from a black and silver flash he could only assume was Willy's cane. Then, out of the corner of his swollen eye, he saw Big Cheeks grab a black case and remove a shiny instrument. He raised it high above his head and held it there. Suspended in space, it looked like a guillotine. PJ screamed. He was going to be decapitated! By the edge of a trumpet!

"Okay! Okay! Okay!" Made feeble by fear, he threw his hands into the air. "I'll talk. Just don't kill me. Please. I'll tell you whatever you wanna know."

Wild Willy motioned for Big Cheeks to lower the trumpet. "Really? Whatever we want?"

PJ tried to catch his breath. "If—you promise—not—to—to do me in."

"Done." Willy raised his right hand into the air. "On my honor, I give you my word as a business man."

Taking the same oath, Veronica stepped over to the downtrodden cowboy and forced her sultry eyes in front of his. Without even a kiss this time, she again had him under her control.

"I could never hurt Patrick James," she vowed. "Why, I'd sooner take my own life than that of a strong, handsome, brave, cowboy like you. Now tell me PJ, who is your partner?"

"Albert." PJ's answer was immediate and without feeling. "Albert E. McTweed."

Willy gave his consent, motioning for Big Cheeks and Sideburns to drag the informant upstairs and throw him out of *his* saloon, which they did—face first into a pile of manure. At his further request, Veronica then brought him a phone, promptly dialing the secret basement of their warehouse.

Al Godón answered. Willy's brother, Charlie, was there, too. The call was placed on speaker phone.

"We've been found out," Willy reported. "We caught someone eavesdropping on our secret meeting. A cowboy named PJ McDougal. There was no sign of his partner. But we cannot be too sure he did not hear us either. Have any of you ever heard of a cowboy named McTweed? Albert E. McTweed?"

Albert buried his face within his arms. His shoulders jerked up and down. "How could you? How could you do this to me, PJ? We were partners. Partners!"

The words cut deep. PJ braced himself against the wall as if faint with the loss of blood. His shoulders sagged under the weight of his burden. He never intended to hurt anyone, especially not his partner. He just...he just...he just didn't know.

And that was the worst part of all. He didn't know why he had done what he had. It was stupid. With a measly kiss, he had betrayed his most trusted companion. And now, for the rest of his life, he was going to regret it.

"Albert. I'm really sorry."

And he was. In fact, PJ had never been sorrier in his whole life. It was a hard thing for him to be and it was a hard thing for him to say, but he meant it. He wished he could take it all back. He wished he could imagine away all of his mistakes. But he couldn't; and it didn't matter what his intentions were, the damage had been done.

"I hate you." It hurt Albert to say it, but at that moment he didn't really care. "I do. And — and I wish you were gone! I — I wish you had never even come here."

PJ's heart stopped. More than the thousand beatings or the countless tortures he had suffered in the name of love and bravery and imagination, these words of Albert's hurt him most of all. But they were all true. And he knew it. He was without excuse. Of his own accord, he had marched into the desert and bared his soul before the elements and been found lacking. And so, with nothing left to say or do, PJ honored this last request of Albert's and left.

A sudden and chilly breeze rushed into the room.

Albert looked up from his arms.

"PJ?"

The curtains in front of his window flapped back and forth. The window was wide open.

Albert looked around.

He was alone.

"PJ?"

He jumped to his feet and ran to the window, leaning out, scanning the horizon until he saw the fleeting movement of shadow. It was Buck. He was galloping toward the setting sun and there, sitting on his back, exerting *all* of his strengths to stay on, urging the bronco onward, was PJ.

"PJ!" Albert screamed into the waning daylight air. "Wait! Come back! I'm sorry. I didn't mean it. I was mad, PJ. That's all. I wasn't thinking. Come back. Please. Please, PJ. I — I — I need you!"

Just then, Albert's door opened and his mom poked in her head. "Hey, you. You ready?"

Albert didn't say anything, but rather sunk to the floor and allowed his mom to come in and sit next to him and give him a great, big hug.

"Come on. It'll be okay." She wiped away his tears, squeezing him again. "The two of you will have fun. I know it. It'll be just like old times. I promise."

17

REFLECTIONS

Upon leaving Albert's room, it took only seconds for PJ to decide that something had to be done and that he was the one to do it. Because if he didn't rescue his good name, he thought, no one would. And if he didn't save his partnership now, then everything they had ever worked for in the past would be but a waste of time and energy.

PJ remembered back to a pair of chaps he had once owned and how they got caught on a nail, and he kept telling himself he was going to patch them up but never did. In the end, the hole got too big, and he had to throw them away. But not this time. Not these chaps. Not this partnership.

"Yaw!"

With encouragement from his spurs, Buck raced PJ ahead: away from Albert's house, through a spider-web of busy streets, over a grassy field, down a series of dirt roads, across a tall mountain range, into the desert, onto the lone street of Dead Dog Crick, and right up to Wild Willy's Motel and Saloon.

"Willy! Big Cheeks! Sideburns! Miss Lux! All of ya, come out with your hands up. I have a piece to speak."

But no one came out at all.

PJ shouted his demands again.

Still, no one answered.

It was then that he noticed a flimsy piece of paper tacked beside the front window.

APOLOGIES TO ALL PATRONS, BARTENDERS, AND SALOON GIRLS:

WILD WILLY'S IS CLOSED UNTIL FURTHER NOTICE. IN CASE OF EMERGENCY, CONTACT OWNERSHIP IMMEDIATELY BY DIALING THE OPERATOR AND ASKING FOR THE SECRET BASEMENT OF BLUE DIAMOND COTTON, INC.

"Blue Diamond Cotton?" PJ scratched his chin. "I don't get it. Why would they be there?"

He looked at the tag on the back of his long johns. Sure enough, they were of the *Blue Diamond* brand. The most comfortable underwear a man could buy. *100% Cotton/100% Algodón.*

"Al Godón?" PJ nearly fell of his horse. He looked back at the tag, quickly putting the ingredients together. "Why, I'll be danged! This whole time he's been runnin' his crime ring out of the secret basement of a cotton company? Holy smokes! And all along I had the clue to it right here on my backside, too."

For a moment, PJ considered removing his long johns in protest. But he decided he'd better wait until he was out of the desert and had an alternate brand to put on. Sand in your jeans was one thing, but sand in them without long johns underneath, why, that brought about a whole different kind of *desert crazies*.

PJ steered Buck over to the burned-out lawyer's office. Inside, on a desk splattered with bullet holes, sat an old-looking phone. The wires were singed and the plastic melted some, but the dial tone rang true. PJ tapped the receiver and asked the operator for directions to *Blue Diamond Cotton*.

"Hold please."

As he waited, he couldn't help but flip over a picture frame resting face-down on the desk. The metal was bent, the glass smashed, and the picture half-burnt. But he could still make out the smiling faces of two men; two brothers; two partners in law. The caption read:

>Bartholomew T. and Thaddeus P. Zookenowski
>Partners Again
>New York Grand Opening

The operator came back to the phone with the requested directions and PJ scribbled them down.

"Ma'am," he shouted back at the phone as he raced out the door and jumped onto Buck, "I 'preciate your help."

With a light tap to the ribs, Buck galloped back through the desert, over the hills, down the roads, across the fields, onto the freeway, and into the vicinity of BLUE DIAMOND COTTON, INC.

"Whoa, boy. Whoa."

PJ pulled the reins taut. Buck skidded to a stop. Towering in front of them was an enormous gateway covered in barbed-wire. Bolted to the front, a less-than-hospitable company sign warned all trespassers to steer clear.

> BLUE DIAMOND COTTON, INC., it read in English
> with a Spanish translation below.
> THE ELEGANCE OF DIAMONDS.
> THE COMFORT OF COTTON.
> ONE LESS EMPLOYEE THAN YESTERDAY.
> **TRESSPASS AND DIE!**

"Shoot. They ain't gonna scare me. Heck no!"

Buck neighed in agreement.

"Thanks, pal. I'll show 'em, all right. I'm gonna make things right, Buck. For real this time. I'm gonna chew up this pickle of all pickles and spit it right back in their faces. Sure as shootin'. For sure, for sure."

PJ dismounted, looking beyond the gates and past the long, paved driveway to a magnificent glass building. Around back he could see a parking lot. A white delivery truck pulled up next to two shiny black cars. With a honk of the horn, several masked workers emerged from the building and began loading chalk boards into the trailer. Out of another vehicle, several white five-gallon buckets were unloaded into the building.

"This has gotta be it." PJ tied the bronco's reins off to the side of the gate and slipped through the bars. "Sorry, Buck. This one I've gotta do on my own."

Buck pawed the ground anxiously but snorted that he understood. He watched his rider tip-toe across the lot and toward the building until he couldn't see him anymore.

PJ waved farewell to Buck as he stepped around the far corner. A courtyard of considerable size occupied the entire side of the building. Scattered across it with apparently no pattern whatsoever were several small, cement lunch tables. Covered in shadow from the setting sun, they looked like gravestones in a cemetery. PJ shivered. Instead of walking through them, he detoured to the left and began making his way toward the end of the break area, where a tall glass sculpture of a blue diamond hovered above a silver fountain of water.

At the pool's edge, he kneeled down and scooped a refreshing handful of water into his mouth. It wasn't soda, but it was cold and it soothed his throat as well as any glass of the finest home-made Sarsaparilla ever had. He wiped his mouth, looking at the hundreds of pennies kids had tossed into the fountain. He wondered what they had wished for and if their wishes ever came true. He wondered what Albert might wish for. Then he gave thought to his own desires. He thought of all that had ever mattered to him. He thought of the girl he once loved... and still loved. He thought of the mistakes he'd made and the right choices he hadn't.

He looked at his strange reflection, wavering among the wind-tossed ripples. He barely recognized himself anymore. His face was dirty. His eyes were tired. His mouth...

He smiled.

Even that wasn't as bright as it used to be.

He turned his eyes to the moon's reflection. For the moment, it was faint. But soon, after the sun had set and the sky turned dark, it would be as bright as anything ever was. By its light, parents would lay their kids to sleep, cowboys would plan their next day's adventures, and weary travelers would plot their courses home.

Out of reverence, PJ removed his hat. He leaned over and ladled another drink. The calm water rippled under his hand. But this time, when it steadied, he was not alone.

Standing behind him, like an angel of death, was a man in a black pin-striped suit. In the light of dusk, the infamous scar on his face glowed purple. With a crooked smile, he reached into his pocket and removed a small handful of white powder.

"*Señor* McDougal," his soft voice hissed. "You're tardy. We've been waiting for you a long time now. We need to know where Albert is going tonight."

PJ jumped back from the fountain. "Why you no-good, low-down—. Never! I have a bone to pick with you Godón. And your gang, too! I intend to make right my wrongs tonight." He thumped his chest valiantly. "Right here. Right now. Or die tryin'!"

"Oh. I see. Well, my foolish *vaquero*[32], I am sorry I am going to miss your grand finale, then. I never stick around, though." His voice lowered to a whisper. "It's the only way to keep from being caught. But if you like, you can take your heroic plans up with *them*."

The mob boss looked over his shoulder to one of the cement lunch tables on the right side. It was then that PJ saw the others. They had been there the whole time. Wild Willy, Big Cheeks, Sideburns, Veronica Lux; even the man in army fatigues. But there was someone else, too; someone immediately familiar to PJ.

"Hey!" PJ pointed to the new face. "Aren't you — ?"

And with that, Al Godón leaned over and blew the powder from his hand into PJ's face.

PJ coughed once, then his eyes closed, and his body toppled onto the courtyard below.

Thump!

18

Making Wishes

Thu-thump. Thu-thump. Thump, thump, thump...

The melancholy beat of car tires on pavement increased to a somewhat frantic whining as Albert and his mom picked up speed, cruised down the on-ramp, and merged into a steady flow of traffic. An emerald-green interstate sign whizzed by. Albert's mom looked at her son and smiled.

"We'll be there soon." She rustled his hair with her fingers. "It's going to be kind of strange seeing the old house again, huh?"

The old house. *Their* old house. Albert had loved that house. Up until last year it was the only one he had ever known. Sometimes...lots of times, he wished they had never moved.

"I know your dad's excited to be with you."

Albert didn't say anything. Instead, he began scribbling on a piece of stationary. Letters and stick figures took their places on the blank stage below.

His mom sighed. "How're you doing, Albert?"

Albert shrugged his shoulders. He wished she wouldn't ask that question anymore. He wanted her to ask him about something else. Like school. Anything, really. Just not *that*. Because he didn't know what he felt anymore. Not really.

Biting his bottom lip, Albert watched the sun disappear behind the hills. But as soon as it was gone, he wished for it back. He felt lonely without it. Alone. Was that how he felt? Is that how he was supposed to feel? Was that what his mom wanted to hear?

With awful clarity, Albert reflected back on the recent events of his life. The horrors of the week passed the window of his mind like slow cars on the freeway, but none more terrifying or painful than the whole ordeal with his partner.

For what seemed like a brief moment in his young life, Albert had known what it meant to be part of a real and meaningful partnership. But now, keenly, he felt the bitter sting of the void left behind in the wake of betrayal. And though his partner had been sincere in his apology, Albert wondered if he could ever bring himself to trust *him* again.

Did he dare chance getting hurt all over again? Would it take but another glance or kiss or whiskey from this Veronica Lux before his partner would betray him again?

Albert squeezed his eyes shut. In the darkness of his mind, he wandered past the tragedies of the week, out of the night and into the comfort of daylight, to a time when things were simple, to a time when things were happy. He breathed in deeply. Oh, how he longed for those days again...

And just like that, Albert had them — all at once: a thousand experiences, a thousand emotions, a thousand smells and touches and tastes and sounds and sights; all merged into a giant rainbow of memory, stretching its arms across time and space.

As if he were there, Albert watched his dad mow the lawn outside their old house. The fresh smell of cut grass filled the springtime air...

Then, almost immediately, that vision vanished and a new one began. The clank of tools echoed off the garage walls. Albert handed his dad a wrench. The summer heat was unbearable, but he loved helping his dad fix the car. His mom brought out two glasses of lemonade.

"For my men," she said. "So you don't shrivel up under the hot sun. Look at it. It looks like an orange on fire, don't you think?"

Agreeing, Albert took the glass. But as he took a drink, his glass cup changed into a mug, and what had been sweet and refreshing was now a rich and hot chocolate—perfect for the blustery fall day. Albert put down his mug, then crunched his way across the leaf-covered ground and began raking them into one big pile, until, that is, a jovial call for help from inside the house interrupted his work. Gladly, he abandoned the leaves and ran into the living room. His dad was wrestling his mom to the floor. They were laughing.

"Help," she cried out. "Save me, Albert. Save me!"

"Don't even try," Albert's dad warned, tickling his lovely prisoner on the neck. "I have her in my *Super Deadly Death Grip of Power*. There's no saving her now."

But Albert was not afraid. With a bold promise to rescue his mom, he climbed the ropes and jumped into the ring. Soon, happy-tears were falling from all of their eyes.

Albert wiped his eyes but only to see snow falling when he took his hands away. He watched his breath crystallize upon leaving his mouth and nose. The wonderful crispness of winter rushed over his body. Then a snowball pelted his backside. Turning around, he watched in giddy horror as his dad charged full-steam-ahead, a collection of snowballs within his arms.

"Take this, you yellow-bellied scoundrel!"

A large snowball zipped past Albert's ear.

"Ah hah! And this, and this, and this..."

"Albert? What are you smiling about over there?"

Albert opened his eyes. It was dark outside. His mom flashed a half-smile as she turned on her blinker and exited the freeway.

"We're almost there."

"Already?"

"Just a few more minutes. Starting to look familiar?"

Albert looked out his window. As they progressed down the off-ramp, the darkness outside lessened. Tall street lamps appeared, dotting the sides of the road every few feet or so, leading the way home. As they drove under them, a momentary shower of golden light lit up Albert's face and the inside of the car. Light then dark, light then dark, then light again…

Soon, several stores came into view. As Albert's mom turned a corner, he saw his old school too, followed not-too-much-later by a row of houses that were as familiar as anything had ever been. Looking at them, it was as if he were greeting again a group of close friends — friends he had never really had before… except for…

And just like that, Albert knew exactly how he felt.

He wiped at his eyes with the end of his sleeve. "Mom," his voice quivered. "Mom, I'm scared."

With one hand on the wheel, Albert's mom pulled her son as close as she could. "I know," she said, fighting back her own tears. "I know. I'm scared, too." Gently, she turned the wheel; and with it the hands of time seemed to turn back, too. She steered the car around one last corner. The headlights lit up a familiar road. "We're here," she said. And they were.

Honk! Honk! Ho-onk!

Albert scooted to the edge of his seat. He looked up at his mom, but she didn't dare return his gaze. Not this time. It was taking all of her strength to keep her focus on the road.

She placed her foot on the brakes and eased into a long, thin driveway with a familiar house at the end. Their old house.

Where they used to live. Where things had been good. Where things had always been happy.

"We're here," Albert's mom said again.

The car rolled to a stop. Silence ensued. Albert's heart quickened its beat and his mouth went a little dry.

"We're here," she said a third time.

She squeezed the back of Albert's neck. A warm shiver ran through his body. The outside-light on the house flickered on, and the front door opened. Against the backlight from the inside, the silhouette of *a man* stepped onto the small, cement porch and waved.

"Here you go, son." His mom's whisper was almost inaudible[33] now. She handed him his bag from the back seat, nudging him along. "Have a good time, okay? I love you. Okay?"

Albert looked up at his mom. In the porch light, her eyes and cheeks were glistening. He gave her a kiss goodbye. Her cheek tasted salty and yet... it was as sweet as candy.

"Okay, Mom." He hugged her and kissed her cheek again. "I will." Then he opened the car door, stepped out onto the grass, and began to make his way up the driveway.

The shadowy figure of his dad knelt to the ground and greeted him at the porch with a pause and then an enormous hug. He didn't let go for a really, really long time. But when he finally did, he took his son's hand in his and rose to his feet — taller than he had stood in quite some time.

A giant and a little boy. *Their* little boy.

Albert's dad raised his other hand, as high and as long as he could, and waved to Albert's mom. Her eyes closed. She nodded to herself then nodded again as she backed out of the driveway and drove off.

Albert and his dad watched her car until the tail-lights were no more than tiny sparkles in the distance, the first twinkling stars shining through the blackest of nights.

Albert made a wish. So did his dad.

Star light, Star bright. First star I see tonight…

Albert looked up at his dad. His eyes and cheeks were glistening, too.

"C'mon," he sniffled. "You hungry?"

Albert said that he was starving.

"Good," his dad laughed. "Me too."

And with that, they stepped into the house… together.

19

UP AND AT 'EM

That night, Albert sat on his bed for quite some time looking at the picture of him and his dad fishing. Lost in the memories of the outing, he could still smell the wonderful stink of fish and feel on his face the cool breeze rolling off the lake. At the time he didn't want to stop fishing, and he remembered being sad when they pulled away. Now, he didn't want to stop looking at the picture, but he wasn't sad.

Albert placed the picture back on the nightstand and turned off the lamp. As he allowed his head to rest on the soft feather pillow, he couldn't help but wonder what his mom was doing. And sometimes, especially during those sleepy moments when dream and reality often blur, he couldn't remember if she wasn't really in the room across the hall after all.

Albert tugged at the covers, nestling them under his chin. When he lived here before, he used to lie awake for what seemed like hours listening to his dad snore. Tonight was no different. The comforting rhythms of his dad's snores were as good as a lullaby. And in their presence he felt safe.

Albert relaxed. His eyes grew heavy, then heavier still, and then he fell fast asleep. A sleep so deep he didn't even stir when his dad awoke to kiss him him goodnight one last time. A sleep so deep, in fact, he didn't even flutter when his window then slid open and in climbed a grotesquely tall man with red hair and wild sideburns.

The clumsy brute stepped across the floor to Albert's bedside and looked upon the sleeping boy. A greedy grin lit up his monstrous mug.

"Albert," he sang creepily. "It's time to wake up. I's come to tell you's a bed-time story."

He placed his dirty hand over Albert's mouth and nose so as to entirely block his breathing. It worked. Albert's lungs struggled for air. His eyes opened. Face to face with a cold-blooded killer, he screamed, or rather he tried to scream, but his muffled plea for help reached no further than the filthy ears of Sideburns Magraw.

"Hello, Albert. We's meet at last! I've come to take you's on a li'l field trip. We's already got yer stupid cowboy friend, y'know?"

In retaliation, Albert opened his mouth and bit down — hard — into the soft flesh below his kidnapper's thumb.

"Arrgghh!"

Sideburns withdrew his hand. Across his palm, tiny drops of blood filled the indentations that were Albert's teeth marks. Like a savage beast, he sucked them dry. Then he grabbed his gun and in a flash of fury slammed it down over Albert's skull. There was a loud *crack*, and Albert's head toppled to the side.

"Sweet dreams, you's li'l brat!"

Sideburns shoved Albert's unconscious body into a grey gunny-sack and tossed it out the window. On cue, a black car pulled up along side the house. The passenger window rolled down, revealing the scarred face of Al Godón.

"*Vayamos*," he shouted. "*Prisa*."

Flustered by Godón's impatient tone, Sideburns struggled through the window. His boots knocked over the picture of

Albert and his dad fishing. Then a piece of paper fell from his pocket and landed next to the bed. He tumbled to the ground below.

"Gosh dangit, Al." He brushed himself off. "You's know I's don't speak no *es-pan-yol.*"

Al Godón rolled his eyes. "Just get in the car!"

Sideburns obeyed but was only half-way in when Godón ordered the driver to drive, and the car sped off toward the warehouse.

Hours later, as the sun was poking its head over the horizon, Albert's dad entered the room.

"Rise an' shine, son. Up an' at 'em, partner. Breakfast is — Albert?"

He looked at the empty bed. He looked at the open window. His eyes fell to a picture on the floor; *their* picture; the one he had set out for Albert the night before. He jumped over to it and picked it up. The glass was broken, and the picture scratched. Careful not to scratch it anymore, he shook the glass from the frame and placed it back on the nightstand. It was then that he noticed something else, a crumpled piece of stationary lying against the base of Albert's bed.

His fingers trembled as he turned it over. A familiar logo of a blue diamond adorned the top. Underneath it, someone had scribbled directions to his house. Next to those directions was a rough drawing of the house with a squiggly arrow pointing right at Albert's window. And finally, in the middle of the page — dead center — three crude stick figures with x's for eyes dangled from a row of equally elementary gallows. Above each, respectively, were the letters: P J then A L B E R T then P A R T N E R S.

Albert's dad gasped. Someone had taken his son! Someone had kidnapped his partner!

From across the room, he looked at the open window again. In the upper section, he could see his own reflection staring back at him. 'What are you waiting for?' it seemed to shout in his direction. 'Giddy up, cowboy! Save the day!'

Albert's dad looked back at the stationary. His eyes narrowed with resolve. What he was about to do was going to be really hard. But he had to do it. Because he loved — really loved — who he was going to do it for.

"Patrick," he reminded himself as he grabbed his cowboy hat from a table in the hallway, "you can do hard things. There's always a way. Always."

20

THE BEARDED CUB SCOUT

As the heavy iron door scraped across the cold cement floor, a sliver of light pierced the otherwise dark prison cell. Principal Klinger stepped into the doorway.

"Hurry," he demanded. "Open the bag."

Stepping up beside him, Sideburns tore at the bag's ties with his teeth and flipped it upside down. Albert's half-conscious body spilled onto the floor.

"I didn't dodge bullets for you to pry into other people's business, boot. Here you'll pay for your eavesdropping, just like your partner is paying for his. There's nothing a little time in the detention barracks can't beat out of anyone."

With that reminder, Klinger turned and exited the prison cell. Behind him, Sideburns shut the door and locked it. Albert listened to their footsteps trail off as they walked down a hallway and up a steep flight of stairs. In the distance, a door slammed shut.

With great effort, Albert rolled onto his side and sat up. It hurt. His entire body felt like he'd been run over by a truck, especially his head. The blood surrounding a large bump on the crown of it had scabbed, but the bruise ran deep. Still more painful was the fact that PJ had been imprisoned, too.

For the first time in Albert's life, he was absolutely partnerless. Because of PJ, they were now both going to die here. The problem was Albert didn't even know where *here* was.

Rising to his feet, he took the opportunity to have a look around. The prison cell was dark and damp, and the walls bulky. It was as if the room had been dug out of the earth by hand. A makeshift bed of blackened hay festered in one corner, and in the other, a poisonous pile of chalk dust. Albert shuddered at the sight and was about to turn away when a third something caught his eye; a dirty strip of cloth entangled in the hay.

However, it was not the cloth alone that intrigued Albert but the fact that it was swaying back and forth from the end of a piece of hay — as if a hurried retreat had torn it from another prisoner's raiment[34].

Albert crawled onto the hay and fingered the cloth. It was warm. He looked back at the bed and ran his hands along the large indentation where someone had once slept. It too was warm.

"Hello?" His voice jittered as he peered into the darkness beyond the bed. "Is — is someone here? PJ? Is that you?"

There was no answer.

"Hello? PJ?"

Still no answer.

Albert closed his eyes, changing his focus instead to the noises around him. He heard water dripping from a crack in the ceiling while a rat's sticky paws pitter-pattered across the stony floor behind him. Then a fly began to buzz around the room. Landing on his head, it greedily explored the bump on it, until, somewhere in the far-off distance, a door slammed shut and scared it away. Albert jumped too.

For several moments after, he heard only the frantic beating of his heart and the sporadic panting of his lungs. To calm his nerves, he drew in a deep breath and held it. But to his surprise, the sound of breathing continued elsewhere. His lungs began to burn as he continued holding his breath, listening with increased awareness to the tranquil aspirations[35] as they grew in strength and volume. They were coming from the corner. They were coming from beyond the bed of hay!

Albert's eyes burst open, scrutinizing again the shadows he had previously searched in vain. But this time, he did see something. He saw movement. A darker shadow in the shape of a man flinched, and a dirty bare foot stepped into the light.

Albert's heart renewed its apprehensive beating. Other than this one foot, the rest of the stranger remained concealed by the darkness, but it was clear to Albert that this was not his partner. Was it one of the criminals then? Were they going to kill him, he wondered, like they had Ms. Hogsteen? Is that how he was going to pay for his supposed eavesdropping — with his life?

"Please," Albert pleaded. "Whatever it is, get it over with."

The bare-footed man sighed. His pause seemed like an eternity. But then he spoke; his voice matured by suffering and solitude; his wisdom increased through countless hours of meditation.

"I mean you no harm," he said, clearing a sickly cough from his throat. His voice was soft and peaceful. "I am friend to all who make this their home."

"Who are you?" Albert shifted to his knees. "How long have you been here? Is there no way out? If you're my real friend, show yourself. Please."

The stranger took another step closer. Forged in the mists of Albert's imagination, a long, frazzled, graying beard came into view. Like a stick of moldy cotton candy, it hung down just below his waist. Without hesitation at all now, the man continued

forward, one step at a time, until the whole of his countenance had cleared the darkest barriers of shadow. Skewed by the passage of time, the shredded remains of a faded, badge-less Cub Scout shirt clung to his bony torso.

Albert looked up at the man's strange face—worn and tired—then deep into his kind eyes; and in their reflection he saw something...someone...familiar. Albert's eyes nearly exploded with astonishment.

He jumped to his feet and ran to the bearded Cub Scout, looking beyond the ratty hair and the dirty rags and the leathery skin. It wasn't a man after all. It was a boy, a boy hidden from the real world by an imaginary beard. It *was* him! *He* was alive!

In a million years, he never could have imagined he'd see him again. Yet here he was, standing in front of him — his long-lost friend. It had been only a year since that fateful day in the gym. To Albert, though, it seemed as if decades had passed.

But now, all that lost time didn't matter anymore. And it seemed as if they had never really been apart at all.

21

THE DESERT CRAZIES

Wild Willy stared into a large one-way window, his cane tapping the floor with childish impatience. From behind him, Veronica promenaded across the room, the long train of a glamorous red dress trailing behind her. Around her neck, a real diamond necklace boasted its magnificence. She tapped Willy on the shoulder.

"My, my," he gawked. "You are too cruel, my dear. Too cruel, indeed."

She smiled. "How's our cowboy doing?"

Willy turned his attention back to the large window. Inside a room the size of an airplane hangar, a jury-rigged[36] desert stretched from each of the four corners. Painted blue, the walls and ceiling resembled a beautiful clear day. A series of hot halogen lights represented the sun, heating the Joshua trees and the hundreds of yards of imported desert sand below. A spotted lizard scurried in front of the window; a rattlesnake followed suit; and there, waist deep in a dune of sand like a boy in a kiddy pool, sat PJ McDougal.

"Hey," he suddenly shouted to no one in particular, his cheeks red with shame. "Did the water just get warmer in here?"

Willy looked back at Veronica and rolled his eyes. "He's getting *there*. Foolish cowboy. Trying to track us down and...what did he say?"

"Make right his wrongs. Kind of sweet, if you ask me."

"That is precisely why I did not ask you, my dear."

As Willy and Veronica continued to monitor PJ's progression, Principal Klinger stepped around the corner and joined them.

"Well, *he's* in the detention cell. Practically out cold, too."

"Good work, brother," Willy replied. "That's one less irritant to worry about. We'll deal with him soon enough. I think we're almost ready here, though." He glanced at his watch. "A few more minutes, no doubt, and he'll be yours, Veronica. It's taken a long time for the desert crazies to set in. Peculiar. He's stronger than we anticipated."

Principal Klinger looked through the window into their *Desert Room* just in time to see PJ scoop up a pile of hot sand and dump it over his head.

"Whooee!" Eyes closed, PJ let the sand run down his face like water. With a devious grin, he turned to his left and proceeded to splash a nearby Gila monster. "Feels real good, don't it?"

"Reminds me of a comrade of mine," Principal Klinger observed, remembering back to a time he and a companion became surrounded by the enemy during a routine scouting mission. "We were trapped in a muddy fox hole for two weeks with nothing to eat but the mosquitoes we could catch. We'd wait until they had sucked our blood. Then right before they took off — splat!" Klinger slapped his arm then scraped the invisible carnage from his skin and licked it off his fingers. "*Ummm — mmm*. Tasted just like chicken. But juicier."

Veronica cringed.

"By the time we got out though, my partner was as batty as the devil. Kept telling everybody he was the commander-in-chief — even after the enemy captured him! Walked right out into the killing field with his hands raised high to the sky and told them to 'stop all of this ridiculous fighting and kiss and make up.' Well, that was the first and last address he ever made." Klinger threw his head back and laughed. "Ah, the good ol' days." He watched as PJ sidled up to the same Gila monster and slipped his arm around its back. "What's he doing now?"

"Well." Willy checked his watch again. "If I'm not mistaken in my understanding and the timing of the so-called *desert crazies*, I believe he thinks he is in a pool with a bevy of beautiful cowboys and cowgirls. And in bathing suits, at that."

Veronica purred with delight. "I should have brought my suit."

Charlie looked her over, scrutinizing the luxurious fabric draped around her. "You mean that's not your suit? I don't think he'll mind."

As the Gila monster retreated, PJ dove into the sand and tickled the toes of a smaller lizard with spots. Flinging it onto his shoulders, he jumped to his feet and began dancing around the room. The lizard looked like it was going to throw up. And it might have, had PJ not stopped to steal a kiss from the mirage of a woman by the side of the pool. Placing his arm around the air to his right, he turned toward the window to introduce her to his friends.

Veronica ducked. "Can he see us?"

"Better not be able to," Charlie huffed. "We forked over a good five thousand dollars worth of fake diamonds for each window in this underground bunker. They're one-way."

"In fact," Willy added, "from the inside this doesn't even look like a window at all. Scientists studied the Chameleon when designing them. They take on the same color as the walls around them."

Playfully, PJ swatted the air. "Get outta here, you silly." He swatted the air again. "Really? Me? You?" He shrugged his shoulders, teetering back and forth like a drunk in a back-alley. "Okee-dokee." Who was he to argue with a beautiful woman anyway? "As you wish." Without further ado, he puckered his lips and pressed them up against the window, kissing it long and good.

Principal Klinger grabbed his stomach as if he'd been shot. "Aagh! Idiot cowboy. I didn't dodge bullets to see that."

"None of us did, good brother." Willy ushered Veronica to the door. "I think that's your cue, my dear. Any longer and he'll be tipping back glasses of hot sand. And he's no good to us dead. Not yet at least."

Willy opened the door. On a metallic plate fastened to the front were the words: *Death Valley*. Like a movie star, Veronica took the stage.

"Ohhh PJ," she called from across the desert in her most seductive voice. "Ohhh Patrick James. Over here, cowboy."

PJ retracted his kiss and raised a finger to the lip-prints on the window. "Don't go nowhere now, you hear? Hold them thoughts. I'll be back in a jiffy."

But as soon as he laid eyes on the woman calling his name, he completely forgot about his promises to the mirage.

PJ wiped the sand from his sunburned eyes. "Miss Lux?" He stumbled forward. "Sure as shootin'! Veronica, it is you. Why, how in the heck did you get here?" He looked up at the sky. He hadn't heard any crop-dusters fly by. "Well, I'll be darned. I sure as heck din't expect to see you — not here in the desert. We have ol' times to catch up on. C'mon, let's find some shade." He pointed to the ceiling. "'Cause that there sun's a real killer." He looked at her dress. "'Bout as hot as your outfit, I reckon. Holy smokes! You don't know what that does to me."

Veronica tapped his nose and smiled. "Why don't you tell me?"

PJ didn't have to think twice. With another "Okee-dokee," he plopped down in the sand to begin.

"No," Veronica twittered, tugging at his arm to help him up. "Not here. Somewhere... else. Somewhere..." Her fingers waltzed down his chest. "A little more *comfortable*."

PJ looked into her eyes — all hypnotic and wild-like — and a mischievous smile spread from one ear to the other. "Yeeehaw! Veronica Lux, I do like the way you think. Ladies, gents," he shouted back at a group of rattlers basking in the sun on a nearby rock. "I've gotta go now. It's been real fun. We'll do it again sometime. For sure, for sure."

Veronica extended her hand. PJ took it in his.

"Hot desert ain't no place for a woman as *pertty* as you, anyhow." Veronica agreed.

"Dangerous, too. There can be snakes in the desert, you know?"

Veronica placed her hand over her heart. "Oh really?"

"You betchya. Lots of 'em. Big, giant, poisonous ones, too."

"Thank you then," she swooned, "for saving me."

PJ slapped his thigh. "Ah, shoot. Any time, any time. That's what us real cowboys do best — we save people. 'Sides you woulda done the same for me."

"Oh, yes," she said as they stepped out of the *desert* and into the hallway. "Of course I would."

In the hallway, PJ paused to inhale a breath of cool air. "Ahhh. You were right, Miss Lux. This is much more comfortable here. Say, what's the occasion anyhow?"

"Oh, you'll see." Casting a wink in the direction of Willy and Charlie, she led PJ down another hallway. "I have something I need you to do for me. Something really important."

"Then I'll do it! Name the deed, and it's as good as done. Sure — as — shootin.'"

Veronica stopped. "Shooting, huh?" Tapping her cheek, she considered the option. "Not a bad idea. A little cliché though, don't you think?"

PJ shrugged. He really didn't know what she was talking about. He just liked to hear her talk. "Whatever you say, Miss Lux. Just keep on a-talkin.'"

Veronica leaned in and kissed him on the cheek. "You're so sweet. Now, don't you worry your handsome little head about a thing. We already have a different method in mind."

22

Always a Way

After recounting his own story, Albert sat down at the feet of Joey Kornwallace and listened to him chronicle the horrid events that occurred once outside the emergency exits of the Elderwood Elementary gymnasium that terrible day in the fifth grade.

"I was then dragged to this basement and locked in this cell to spend the remainder of my days." Joey looked around as if the dark abode had begun to grow on him. "With nothing to eat," he added in a voice dripping with despair, "but one piece of grape bubble gum."

"Per meal?"

Joey removed a purple wad from his mouth and tossed it to the side. Oh, how he despised the taste of grape gum now. "No," he clarified, suppressing a cough. "One piece of gum a day."

"A day?" Albert stared at the slimy wad on the floor. "And you've been here ever since?"

"Regretfully so."

"But Joey," Albert refuted with optimism foreign to them both, "you're alive! You didn't die. We all thought you had died!"

Joey bowed his head. A violent cough seized his lungs. "Sometimes...I wish I had. You don't know the tortures that await you if you stay, Albert. One day, after a particularly brutal beating, I begged Principal Klinger to take my life. But he denied my request, saying I would be getting off much too easy if he were to end it early. 'No,' he said. 'I'd rather see you suffer a little longer. I dodged bullets so you could learn, not stick gum on my chair. Because of you the whole school saw me in my skivvies! No,' he denied my request again. 'I'm afraid the embarrassment you caused me is far too fresh in my mind for an early dismissal.' He told me he'd seen P.O.W.'s hanged for less. In gruesome detail, he described their suffering; the panic in their eyes and faces; the agony of their screams; the names of loved ones on their trembling lips; and then the awful silence that followed."

Albert ground his teeth together. "That monster!"

"Yes, but..." Joey pointed to the pile of chalk dust in the corner. "Out of mercy, he did leave me that, saying if I chose a faster way out, it would be fine with him. Believe me, Albert, on more than one occasion I considered giving in to that pile."

"But you can't," Albert pleaded. "No. Don't do it, Joey. It's not worth it. There's got to be a way out of here."

"Yes. There is." Joey paused, reflecting upon the one way of escape he knew and the hope that was its early foundation. The somber grey in his face lessened. "Forgive me. Long ago the emptiness of solitary confinement slaughtered my hope of a reunion with the outside world. I am having to re-learn the very thing that always kept me going: hope. You are right, Albert. There *is* always a way out...if you put your mind to it. For me, I had to put my back into it as well."

Joey reached behind him. From under the bed of moldy hay, he removed a small wooden box. It stunk of mildew. Albert watched as Joey's shaky fingers slid the lid from its base and withdrew a long, dark dagger of sorts.

"I apologize for the crudeness of the tool. I had only the daily ration of gum I chewed with which to fashion it. One hundred and eighty-some pieces in all. It was quite sticky at first, entirely useless. But as it dried it turned rock hard."

Joey crawled across the room to the wall furthest from the cell door. He jammed the tip of the tool into a small crack and began rocking it back and forth. It took all of the energy he had left; but in the end, an entire section of the wall jarred loose, falling to his lap. He lifted the large round stone and rolled it to the side, revealing a deep cavern jutting back into an unknown darkness.

Albert stared in disbelief at the intricate tunnel. He poked his head inside.

"Joey, you built this?"

"I just finished it this morning." He sighed at the miraculous timing of it all. "You see, Albert, early on in my confinement the thought occurred to me that Klinger might never let me out. I knew I couldn't wait for him to let me out, and I certainly couldn't live my whole life in this dismal cell hoping in vain that he would. It was that fruitless meandering[37] about that near killed all hope and possibility for a better life, you understand?"

Albert thought he did.

"Sometimes in life, Albert, *you* have to *make* things happen. And so that is what I set out to do. When my knife was finished, I spent as much time as I could on the tunnel." He looked at his masterpiece as one would their most trusted companion. "It was hard work. But I kept telling myself I could do hard things. And then, to my surprise, I could. I chipped away at it all night sometimes. It gave me something to live for. And the thought came to me one night that if Principal Klinger should ever take another prisoner it just might give them something to live for, too. It made me strong to think my pain and suffering could make another's lighter. I never could have imagined it would be you." Joey took Albert's shoulder in his calloused hand and gave it an endearing squeeze. "I'm glad you are here, Albert. You were the only one who tried to save me that day in the gym. Seeing you has brought me much comfort and joy... and hope in these my final days."

"Final days? Joey, what are—? We can escape together. There's enough room in there for both of us. Joey, you can live again. You can really live again. Partners don't leave partners behind, Joey. I couldn't hang onto you in the gym last year, but I won't leave you now."

Joey shook his head. A soft smile radiated from behind his imaginary beard. But a second cough—this one more severe than the first—immediately wiped it away. "I am sorry," he choked. "This road you must travel alone. I am sick, Albert. A year with no food... the beatings... the tunnel. It took all of my strength to finish it. I'm afraid it's too late for me." He coughed again. "I will remain here and take the brunt of the punishment for your escape. But you must go. You and you alone have so much to live for."

Albert shook his head. He refused to believe that Joey didn't have something to live for, too. But Joey's mind was made up.

"My choice has been made," he said.

His eyes glistened with emotion. Against his beard, they looked like two stars burning through a covering of dark rain clouds. Albert remembered back to the wish he'd made with his dad.

"Besides, Albert, there is another partnership you must save; another partner who needs your help more than I. It is to him you must go."

Albert bowed his head. "I know," he said. "I know I need to. I—I just don't know if I want to. You know?"

Joey did. "But," he said, "this is not about what we want anymore. This is about what we have to do."

Albert squeezed his eyes shut. His heart struggled. Like the cut on his head, his partner's betrayal was still fresh in his mind. He didn't know what to do. If he tried to do too much too early, he risked the chance of making the pain worse. Then again, if he didn't make clean with it now, he might not get another chance for a really long time. And time, he knew, would only make the neglected sores worsen. The lesions[38] inside his heart would fester until, like Joey — a prisoner of his anger — he would be too weak to escape through the tunnel that was always his to use.

The very idea of wasting away was enough. Without looking back, Albert welcomed to the forefront of his mind the bitter pains and betrayals of his past. One by one, he engaged them in mental battle, and before his superior sword they likewise fell. By the time the dawn in his mind had arrived, the war was finished; and as the sun came up, the bodies of the slain turned to bone then ash then nothing at all.

"I know," Albert whispered. "You're the one who's right this time. I know what I have to do."

"You must hurry, then. There is no telling when Principal Klinger will come back for you."

The two embraced. Joey pulled away first, pushing his friend toward the tunnel like a parent encouraging their child on the first day of kindergarten. Albert ducked his head and crawled inside the tunnel. He looked back at Joey, longing for the comfort of his companionship a little longer.

"You'll be fine," Joey told him. "It'll be dark. But don't be afraid. Follow the tunnel to its end. Once there, feel around. You will find an old school box containing items sufficient for the final leg of your journey. Good luck, my friend."

Albert reached out and grabbed Joey's hands. But then, without fanfare, their grips pulled apart, and the stone, which had once concealed the tunnel, rolled back into place. Darkness consumed the road ahead.

"Joey?"

Albert wanted to hear his voice again. But there was no answer. This time, he was on his own. Staring into the darkness head on, he began his ascent to the end.

Back in the prison cell, Joey secured the stone in place. Having exhausted all of his strength, he crawled over to the bed of hay and lay down. His job was done. A deep sigh released from his lungs a lifetime of burdens. A warm smile brought an angelic glow to his face. Then his eyes closed, and quietly, he slipped away.

23

THE EXIT INTERVIEW

Big Cheeks watched the clock as the workers raced to finish the day's orders. The seconds ticked away, and the minutes passed until finally the big hand and the little hand struck the hour. Big Cheeks blew into the trumpet mouthpiece hanging about his neck. A wheezy shriek whistled from the golden medallion.

"Stop!"

Everyone stopped. Punctual as ever, the outside door opened and a shiny pair of shoes overshadowed by well-pressed pin stripes entered the room. Al Godón wasted no time in getting down to business.

"*Bueno,*" he said as he began inspecting the workers' stations. "*Bueno y bueno y bueno.*"

They were all clean. Smiling, Godón signaled his appreciation. With this latest batch of diamonds, greater political powers than he had ever imagined would be his. And within a few short hours, the only two threats to his diamond empire would be dead. Production and business acquisitions and payroll could again go on as usual — finally.

The news of delayed payment schedules had made several *customers* antsy. The North Koreans were calling for war; Russia's elite were withholding vital information; and the local politicians were threatening to blow the roof of the whole underground operation. They all wanted their money yesterday. But Al Godón was not worried. Not really.

The North Koreans were all bark, and if they decided to bite, the impending war would not be such a bad thing. Even wars could be controlled with money. The Russians would still cooperate, too. They were too poor not to. They needed his diamonds. And as for the locals, they didn't dare expose him. By doing so, they'd implicate themselves. The future of their political and financial and social statuses would be in shambles. The sacrifice of everything they held dear would prove too great. And no one, he told himself, was that noble.

The anxious eyes of every worker locked in on Al Godón as he walked over to the oven and picked up a tray of fake diamonds. Like a teacher reading aloud a student's English paper in front of the class, he inspected every angle of the sparkling blue objects. They looked good.

He moved on to inspect a number of trays cluttering a nearby table. His eyes twinkled. Yes, the allegiances, though threatened, would remain intact. They were his forever...for a price, of course. There was always a price. But still, no price was too high for complete control of the world's upper crust. Nothing could be done without his counsel or approval; no talks could be entered into; no trades solidified; no emergency aid given. A greedy smile engrossed his face, contorting his scar upwards.

And who, he wondered, says crime doesn't pay? Especially when fake diamonds are used.

"*Algo para nada,*" he cackled. "Something for nothing. Beautiful, no?"

"*Sí*," came the obedient reply from each of the workers in attendance. "Of course, *jefe*."

"*Bueno.*"

Godón returned the praise-worthy diamond to its tray and moved over to the last of the diamond batches. From the first row, he picked up the first diamond and dropped it over the floor. A nervous gasp resonated throughout the room. All eyes watched as it tumbled down through the air and hit the floor.

Tink. Tink. Tink, tink, tink, tink…

"*Perfecto.*"

Its shape was precise; its color magnificent. Such brilliance could only be achieved through proper cut and culture. Al Godón picked his invention up from the floor and gave Big Cheeks the thumbs-up.

"*Amigos!*" he shouted, hands high in the air. "*Gracias por su trabajo duro.* You will be rewarded for your hard work."

Like a great big gust of wind, a sigh of relief rushed across the room, and the workers began exchanging handshakes and hugs and congratulations. But as their boss turned to leave, he bumped into a chair accidentally left out. All celebrating stopped. The chair flew into the air and crashed to the floor, skidding across the room. To everyone's horror, Al Godón also went flying into the air. His head smacked the corner of the oven then his back slammed onto the floor.

The room turned silent. From across the laboratory, a middle-aged man in a light blue smock tore the dust mask from his face, pale with fright. His eyes remained fixed on the chair spinning like a child's top. It was his chair. Again!

Al Godón jumped to his feet, fuming like a dragon.

"José!"

His roar echoed off the walls. Big Cheeks raced over to the chalkboard and slashed a piece of chalk beside the corresponding name. A heartsick whimper escaped from everyone's lips.

Uno, dos, tres... Three check marks!

Godón jumped over to the man in question and squeezed his arm. "*Esto no es acceptable!*" he yelled. "Not! Acceptable!"

Like a tremor all in itself, the man's entire body began to shake. "I'm sorry," he blubbered. "I forgot. *Lo siento.* I'm trying. But — but I have problems at home and — and I've had a hard time concentrating. *Por favor*," he begged. "Please forgive me. I need another chance. Please. *Uno mas, uno mas, uno mas...*"

"*Problemas?*" Al Godón questioned, jerking José closer. "At home?"

José sniffled, nodding his head with shame. He looked at the other workers — at his only friends. He hadn't wanted them to know he was having problems at home. He was afraid they would judge him, or think differently of him, or say that he should try harder. But one look in their eyes told him they were not judging him at all. In fact, far from it, their sympathetic minds turned to their own struggles at home. Maybe, they thought, *they* weren't so bad after all. And maybe they should try a little harder, too.

José looked back at Mr. Godón. "*Por favor*," he begged for mercy again. "One more chance. *Para mi familia.* For my wife and my kids."

But Al Godón was beyond family. The desert bandits didn't show any mercy when they robbed and killed his father. And no one came to his aid when the fallout of poverty and starvation reduced his mother to the dust from whence she came. So why should he show mercy to others who enjoy what he cannot?

"*¿Familia?*" Godón abruptly yelled. "*¿Problemas?* We all have problems *at home, José*. But when we bring our *outside* problems *inside*, we create problems *at work*. Problems which you now have! Big Cheeks? *¡Matele!*"

Panic gripped José's face, but Al Godón didn't care. Quickly, he exited the building. And when the door had shut behind him, Big Cheeks blew back into his mouthpiece. Like a dog to a whistle, the interior door on the opposite side of the room swung open and in sauntered Sideburns Magraw. He licked his lips, hungry and anxious.

"Take this fool out back!" Big Cheeks growled. "And do as you please. We have no time for the distracted here."

Like a jack rabbit, José bound into the center of the room. He didn't know where he was going to go, but he thought that if he could just keep running long enough, he might eventually find a way out. Unfortunately, jack rabbits have never faired very well against the coyote, the wolf, or any other animal of the mad dog nature.

Sideburns howled with delight as he grabbed José, his strong hands gnawing at his neck like the jaws of a blood-thirsty beast.

"You can't do this to me!" José yelled, kicking and screaming. "*Mi familia. ¡Por favor!* I love them! Pleeeeease!"

But Sideburns didn't care, either. Across the floor he steamed, dragging José behind him, and through the door they went. A muffled scream fell short, cut down by a loud *bang!* And then there was nothing at all. A few seconds later, Sideburns returned, alone, *hee-ing* and *haw-ing* — one part hyena, one part bull-headed burro.

"That Mexican-speakin' dude screamed like a girl," he squealed, imitating a high-pitched yelp. "Not as high as that dang lawyer fella did though!"

"Sam!" Big Cheeks' censure was quick. "Shut up!"

He was tired of hearing his dim-witted companion reference the late-Counselor Zookenowski. Yes, they had killed him; their first big city lawyer. They tied him to horses and rode off into the desert, then left him for dead among the wild beasts. It was brutal. It was heartless...

"It was in the past!" Big Cheeks' face blew up like a balloon. "So keep it there. 'Cause if you keep braggin' about it, one of these days you're gonna get us all hanged for it!"

There were too many words in Big Cheeks' diatribe[39] for Sideburns' brain to compute, but there was no mistaking his intonations and exclamations. Tail between his legs, Sideburns stepped back through the doorway to await another opportunity to *fire* a worker with his six-shooters. As the door swung shut behind him, Big Cheeks turned to the employees who were now one less than they had been the day before, and directed their attention to José's empty work station.

"Let that be a lesson to all of you," he snarled, pointing at each and every one of them. "We hired you! Not your families working the plow across the border. So leave them where they belong. At home!"

Instantly though, in direct defiance of Big Cheeks' orders, everyone in the room turned their thoughts to home.

24

Light at the End of the Tunnel

Albert felt his way through the dark tunnel. The air was stale and dusty. The floor's hastily chiseled edges dug at the flesh on his hands and knees. A jagged rock scraped the back of his head and when he went to soothe it, he cut his hand on the same sharp point. He cursed the darkness.

He recalled a period in his life when he had been scared of the dark. He'd wake up in a cold sweat and run into his mom and dad's room and ask to sleep with them. But they never let him — not for long anyway. Usually, after only a few minutes, his dad would pick him up and carry him into his room. He'd place him on his bed and tuck the covers under his chin then tell him a story and say 'it's okay, everything will be okay.' 'The monsters in the dark are just make-believe', he'd say, 'and you can imagine them away any time you want.' He told him to think of happy things instead, like baseball and friends and fishing. It worked. Then one day, Albert got a nightlight. And that worked, too. It was so much easier to sleep with a nightlight.

Albert wished he had one now. He sucked in a deep breath of air as he wriggled his body through a particularly tight spot in the tunnel. Onward, he went. He had no real sense of time in the darkness, but it seemed like he had been crawling forever. Where, he wondered, was the end? And would it ever end?

Thunk!

Albert's head collided into a wall of stone. He had reached the end.

His eager hands patted the ground around him, overturning a rock, some dust, and finally a box. He knew it had to be the school box Joey had told him about. He slipped his hands under the lid and felt inside. There was a paper object of some kind, a pair of scissors, a ruler, some paste, some more paper, and...a flashlight!

Albert grabbed it and pushed the button on the side. A brilliant light illuminated the immediate tunnel around him. The building's vents formed a second tunnel just above his head. In front of him, simple chalk drawings decorated the wall, depicting Joey's sad story in its entirety. He would not be lost after all, Albert thought. The drawings would preserve the memory of the Bubblegum Martyr forever.

Albert picked up a piece of chalk from the base of the wall. Careful not to inhale its dust, he sketched a final picture of Joey. Unlike the other depictions though, this one was smiling.

He turned his attention back to the school box. Next to the ruler, a red Origami crane brightened the corner — it was very well done — and underneath it was a picture of Joey from the fifth grade.

Albert ran his fingers over the filmy face of his friend. Oh, how he had changed since then. Oh, how they had all changed. Pushing the picture back under the crane, he looked upon the last papery object in the box. A map! His hands shook with excitement. He picked it up. It was as light as tissue paper and just as frail. With great care, he unfolded it, taking the necessary time to smooth its edges over his knee. It read:

CRIMINAL EMPLOYEES ONLY
BLUEPRINTS FOR THE UNDERGROUND FACILITIES OF —.

Albert's eyes swelled. He could scarcely bring himself to read the words that followed; three little words forming the name of a company he suddenly hated more than anything else in the whole world; three simple words representing a business employed by heartless criminals who took away his partner, forcing him to betray all trusts; three seemingly insignificant words:

BLUE DIAMOND COTTON.

More determined now than ever, Albert scanned the intricate layout of hallways and rooms. PJ had to be in one of them, he thought. But which one?

The Secret Sales Room?
The Secret Bathroom?
The Secret Lunch Room?
The Secret Conference Room?
Or...
"The secret basement."

That was it! With the tip of his finger, Albert traced the outline of the room. A secret corridor ran alongside its western wall, conveniently leading to a secret emergency exit.

Albert closed his eyes. Like a drive-in movie, the plan for his partner's rescue played out across the darkness in his mind. He would navigate his way through the building's vents, locate the appropriate room, and rescue PJ — he took the scissors from the box — by whatever means necessary. Then they'd escape back into the vents, traverse[40] the corridor, and run out through the emergency exit.

Albert looked at his watch. There was not much time. Bracing his feet against the rock walls, he boosted himself into the second tunnel. He shined the flashlight ahead. Like the plains of the Old West, an impossible maze of metallic paneling stretched out before him. He turned his light to the map, studiously memorizing the elaborate combination of twists and turns. Tucking the map into his pocket, his teeth clamped over the scissors. With the light in his hand, he crawled ahead.

The path was dark, though compared to the previous tunnel, it was as light as day. Headstrong, he clamored along: down dusty chutes; up ladders covered in cobwebs; over cracked planks; under slippery pipes; and across a long, rickety rope bridge with a river of fire flowing underneath.

Danger seemed to lurk at every corner; booby traps at every step. It was hard — real hard, but in Albert's mind his goal was clear and nothing was going to stop him now. Onward he persevered until the tunnel's steep inclines and drop-offs plateaued, and he found himself just outside The Secret Basement.

A large vent glowed from the light inside.

25

THE FINAL STRUGGLE

No longer needing the flashlight, Albert clicked it off and set it down. It had done its job. The rest was up to him.

Shifting onto his belly, he slid up to the front of the grate and looked through its slotted metal openings into the secret basement. The room was dark and dreary except for a small orange lamp hanging from the high cement ceiling by a rusty chain. Like a streetlamp, it cast its dim glow onto the cement floor below where a metal chair marked **PROPERTY OF ELDERWOOD ELEMENTARY** rocked from side to side with the near-unconscious sways of a man imprisoned. It was PJ. But he was not well.

Bound to his chair by a cowboy's lasso, his hands and legs were raw from chafing[41]. His arms and face bore the bruises of a ruthless beating while his hat, like his ego, was depressed and wilting. But more painful than all of these, was the yellow-brown saliva dripping down the sides of his leather boots. It was headed straight for his sole.

As Albert looked at his partner — alone and hurting — a bitter rush of emotions tried again to vanquish his cause, fear and doubt among the most prominent. Like the vilest of false-accusers and *nay-sayers*[42], they spit in his face and flung mud at his feet. They penetrated the pit of his stomach and flooded the very valves of his heart. But his mind, they could not touch. In the face of their charge, a mighty wall of timber and stone took shape, keeping at bay the catastrophic consequences of their unjust accusations.

Albert closed his eyes, drawing in a deep and methodic breath like a general on the eve of a decisive battle. Hurting or not, that was his partner and this was his chance; this was his war to win or lose; and come what may, he had to win. Because it wasn't just about him anymore; it was about *them* and them alone.

"And partners," he reminded himself under his breath, "don't leave partners behind."

In a flash, Albert flipped onto his back, kicking the grate as hard as he could. It moaned, but bent inward no more than an inch. He brought his knees back to his chest a second time then kicked again with all of his might — then again and again and again.

Clang!

The grate crashed to the cement floor.

"PJ," Albert yelled as he shimmied through the opening. "It's me!" Scrambling to his feet, he raced toward his partner and slid into the base of the chair. "It's Albert. I'm here to rescue you. I'm here partner. I'm here! I've found a way out. Come on."

Unable to say anything, PJ's head rocked to the side in weak acknowledgment. Albert grabbed the scissors from his pocket and thrust their sharp edge into the rope about PJ's legs. Frantically, his hands sawed back and forth like a machine.

"Don't worry, partner. I'll get you outta here. Me and you. Together."

Snap!

The rope around PJ's legs fell to the floor. Blade met rope again, this time around his wrists. Albert sawed like his life depended on it. Perhaps, he thought, it did. Under the scissors' sharp edge, he watched the individual fibers of the lasso give way until they too fell to the floor.

"Yes! You're free. Now come on, partner. Let's get out of here and go —"

As fast as a bullet, PJ's hands shot from his lap and grabbed Albert by the throat, cutting short his plea to go "*hohhhhme!*" Albert's head exploded with immediate pain. Frantically, he grabbed at PJ's fingers in an attempt to pry them loose. But it was no use.

"PJ," he screamed. A terrible gurgling sound bubbled from his lips. "It's — it's — m-m-me. Your — your part — ner."

Partner? PJ refused to make eye contact, but Albert could see the word meant nothing to him anymore. Glazed over by trance, his bloodshot eyes boiled with madness and hatred and pain and lies, lies, lies.

PJ's sand-filled fingernails dug deeper into the skin of his once-beloved partner, breaking off all possible airflow. A painful wheeze rushed from Albert's lungs. In an attempt to rise to his feet and somehow lessen the agony, he kicked at the floor. Instead, the soles of his shoes collided with something metallic, and he slipped back down to his knees. The pair of scissors from Joey's school box slid into his line of sight. Without hesitation, he dropped his hands to the floor and grabbed them, sinking them deep into the back of PJ's hand.

"Let — go!"

But PJ was numb to the pain. He looked at the silvery object protruding from his hand and swore. He grabbed the scissors and tossed them to the cement. Teeth grinding, he lifted Albert into the air and shook him. Like a seal among killer whales, Albert's body flopped back and forth.

"Pleeease," he cried, trying again in vain to wrest[43] his neck from PJ's grip. "It's m-m-me. P-please. Hel-hel-hel…"

Help me, he continued to say, but this time nothing came out. His vision darkened, his hands fell to his side, and his head felt lighter than ever; then his burdens, too. A bright light beamed just ahead, illuminating a third and final tunnel; a tunnel that at once seemed strangely familiar.

Was this *it?* he wondered. Was he on his way *home?* For good?

Albert relaxed. With open arms, he welcomed the idea. But it was not his time yet. For the first time, PJ looked into the eyes of the boy he was killing, then beyond them, and deep into his soul, where he saw something…someone…familiar. He hesitated. Inside, a mighty struggle ensued; a bloody battle raged on. He closed his eyes. He didn't dare open them…because he *had* to kill Albert. Those were his orders. Kill him, they said, no matter what! ¡Matele! ¡Matele! ¡Matele! But…but why?

PJ shook his head, trying to make sense of everything that had happened. He shook it again. "I can't. I…I won't!" In spite of the spell, his eyes opened. And in an instant he knew the boy. "Albert!" He released his grip, but only to have his partner's body crumple to the floor, barely breathing. "Albert?" PJ's shoulders lurched forward, tears roaring down his cheeks; a flash flood in the barren desert. He buried his face into Albert's tiny chest. "No, no — no! Albert. I'm sorry. Please. Come back. Come back to me, please. I don't know what came over me. They had me under some kinda spell again. I din't mean to hurt you, partner. I'm sorry. I need you, Albert. Please. Come back, Albert. Please, oh please, oh please…"

As if summoned from the dead, Albert's body twitched; his chest heaved, a cough seized his lungs, and a loud wheeze rumbled out of his mouth. His lungs took air, his face regained color, and his eyes opened.

"PJ?"

"Yes!" PJ threw his arms around Albert and brought him to his chest, cradling him like he would a newborn son. "Sure as shootin'. I'm here, partner. And I ain't ever gonna leave you again. That's a promise."

But just then, a door burst open, additional overhead lights flashed on, and plotting laughter filled the room.

"Now that's what I dodged bullets for. Best five-thousand dollar investment we ever made."

Having witnessed the entire ordeal from behind a large one-way window, the criminals entered the room. Juggling a piece of chalk in one hand, twisting an army knife in the other, Charlie Klinger marched in first, taking his place at the head of an invisible line. Wild Willy entered the room next, tapping his cane across the floor as he took his brother's side. With a golden trumpet in his hands, Big Cheeks Malone joined them followed by Veronica Lux. The train of her red dress flowed behind her like a river of hot lava. With a wink in PJ's direction, she made way for Sideburns Magraw, who stumbled in after her, spinning his two *Gentleman Six-Shooters* like they were pinwheels from a carnival. But that was not all. Behind him yet another outlaw entered the room...

Albert looked up in horror at this last and unexpected doer-of-foul-deeds; the very one PJ had seen outside in the *Blue Diamond* courtyard; the very one he had thought he recognized from that early morning outside Elderwood Elementary School, classroom D-15. D as in Deceit.

"Miss Lovely?"

26

A Change of Heart

Albert's heart broke into a thousand pieces, sinking, like a giant ocean-liner, to the crushing depths of the ocean floor below.

In its wake, Laura bowed her head, too ashamed to look into the eyes of Albert or his now-triumphant partner. She scurried to the end of the line and fixed her eyes on the floor.

"Bravo!" Wild Willy exclaimed, extending his hand in praise to the partnership in front of him. "That was some show you two put on. I never would have guessed the outcome. Why, up until the end, I thought PJ was going to kill Albert." Willy tapped the handle of his cane over his palm. "At least, that's what was supposed to happen. You see, Albert, we were going to bring you here anyway. Your unexpected escape and rescue just saved us a step is all. My brother here thought it would be fun to watch your partner do you in and I have to admit, he was right. Well, almost. You're not dead, are you? Perhaps, Veronica, the spell didn't have time to really take hold?"

Veronica shrugged her shoulders. Having combined the *desert crazies* with her eyes and her red dress, the spell should never have been broken. It was perhaps the most bewitching tonic of all and, in the heat of the moment, its hold should have continued with PJ until he had taken his partner's life.

"I'm troubled," Willy admitted. "Her powers certainly aren't weakening. I should know. I am her employer, after all. But if not that, then what?" He cast a frustrated glance at PJ. "Perhaps your powers are getting stronger then, eh, cowboy? Perhaps you are a diamond in the rough." From his suit pocket, he removed an opaque[44]cube of blue caked in a white dust of some kind or another. "Questionable on the exterior, but full of brilliance on the inside. Your heart serves you well, Patrick." His hand slipped back inside his jacket from which he removed a silver gun, pointing it at PJ's chest. "Unfortunately, there is no room for heart in the criminal underworld. Say goodbye, cowboy. Your adventure is over."

His finger slipped around the trigger and began to squeeze. But PJ was not going to go down without a fight. He had looked down many a law-breaker's barrel before and sure as shootin' this crude cylinder was nothing to lie down and die before.

He glanced around the room. A glint of silver amidst a tangle of frayed lasso ends caught his eye, and he dove for it. As hand met scissors, he clambered to his feet and whipped them in front of him, jabbing them in Willy's direction.

"I'm warnin' you," he shouted. "You can shoot me if you want, but you sure as heck ain't gonna kill me till I got these here scissors deep in your gullet."

Willy's brow crumpled with immediate concern. He looked at the tiny pair of elementary school scissors. This cowboy, he thought, is as brave as he is foolish. Surely he doesn't intend to challenge my gun with those. But those were PJ's exact intentions and Willy could see that he meant business. Before his wild eyes, the dull scissors seemed to morph into a shiny, sharp saber.

To everyone's surprise, Willy lowered his gun.

"Very well. We'll see just how brave you really are, you insignificant drag-rider[45]. Tie him up."

Charlie leaned forward, pointing at Miss Lovely. "And her, too."

"What?" Miss Lovely sprang from her place in line, but only to be grabbed by Veronica and slammed into the wall. "Let go of me," she yelled, struggling to get away. "This wasn't part of the deal. Let go. You gave me your word. I said let — me — go, you floozy[46]!"

Gasping at the insinuation[47], Veronica took a step back and let her hand fly through the air. There was a loud *slap* followed by a gasp equal in vibrancy. Miss Lovely's chest heaved. Her eyes burned with indignation.

"You!"

Growling like a lioness defending her cubs, she took a commanding step toward Veronica. She was ready to pounce, and would have done just that had not a man first called out to her from across the room.

"Laura." His voice was soft, yet brimming with strength and confidence. "Laura," he said again. "Please, listen to me. It's okay."

Laura stopped. She turned to look at the stranger next to Albert; the cowboy with the collapsed hat and the warm smile on his face.

"Don't struggle," he pleaded. "It'll be all right. Trust me. *Everything'll* be fine. All of us." He pointed to Miss Lovely and Albert, then back to himself. "We'll all be okay."

Laura searched the cowboy's eyes. She didn't know anything about him and yet... somehow... she trusted him. "Okay," she whispered. "Okay." And with that, she closed her eyes and held out her hands for Veronica to tie up.

PJ, too, submitted himself to the whims of the criminals. Big Cheeks slapped the scissors from his hands. Willy hogtied him into the metal chair next to Laura. And Sideburns, never one to think, cleared his throat and launched yet another slimy glob of spit onto the tip of PJ's right boot.

PJ looked down at the spittle as it jiggled its way to the floor. In his heart of hearts, he was a fuming ball of fire, but on the outside, he remained cool as ice. Now, he kept telling himself, is not the time for retaliation. He had to be patient. In time, the right opportunity would present itself. Then Sideburns and all of his criminal cohorts would get their *just deserts*. But not until then.

Biting his tongue, PJ issued a warning glance in Sideburns' direction then turned to officially greet the lady tied up in the chair next to him.

"Ma'am," he bowed his head out of respect. "It's a real pleasure. Wish it were under brighter skies. For sure, for sure."

"For sure nothin'!" Sideburns shouted, shaking his bandaged fist in front of PJ's face. "I's still ain't prop'ly paid you's back fer this here hole in my hand."

Like a bolt of lightning, Sideburns' hand came barreling down from the sky and slammed into PJ's stomach. PJ jerked forward with pain, but only to see Sideburns' boot fly up through the air and tag him in the jaw. His head snapped backwards, a thin stream of blood running from his nose and mouth.

Laura screamed. Albert, too. Jumping to his feet, he ran to help PJ. But, out of nowhere, a violent back-hand sent him reeling back down to the floor.

"And stay down! You's so much as move another muscle, kid, I's a swear I'll knock yer block off. Like this!"

A thunderous boom caught PJ right between the eyes. His head snapped back again and, for a split second, everything around him went dark. His face felt like it was on fire and his head throbbed. But he couldn't let *them* see his pain. Not today, not ever. For their sakes, he had to remain strong.

"I'm okay," he rasped to Albert and Laura. "*Shhhh.* Don't cry ma'am. Everything'll be fine. I'm fine. For sure," he smiled, his teeth stained red with blood, "for sure."

"Again, bravo! Bra-vo!" Willy stepped over to Sideburns and pulled him back. "I've never seen anyone take a hit like that and keep talking. Well done, Patrick. You really are something. I almost hate to see you die." He turned to Laura. "You too, of course, my dear. But especially you, Albert." Like a shark on the scent of blood, he began to circle the boy. "I like you. I really do. Why, anyone who has the audacity[48] to escape from prison and come back for a partner who once betrayed him is a rarity in this world, indeed."

Albert's heart pumped with anger. "I don't care what you think. You're murderers. All of you — murderers!"

"Murderers?" Willy frowned. "*Tsk. Tsk.* That's a bit unfair now, don't you think? We're not all murderers."

"He is." Albert pointed to Principal Klinger. "You killed Ms. Hogsteen! I heard you say it in the bathroom. On the phone with Big Cheeks."

"Wrong," Principal Klinger objected. "If you heard anything, you heard only what you wanted to hear. I never once said I murdered Ms. Hogsteen — because I didn't. In fact, it took three people to do away with that blubbery old hippo that was your teacher." Turning around, he pointed the tip of his army knife in Sideburns' direction. "One," he counted, "to keep her unconscious. Two," he shifted the blade toward Big Cheeks, "to pour the cement around her fat hooves. And three..." Bringing the knife back over his head, he launched it at the third accomplice. "To drive the car to the docks and help push the fat lard into the ocean."

Albert watched in horror as the long, sharp blade sailed across the room and — *thunk!* — impaled itself into the wall not even a centimeter from Miss Lovely's face. A small smattering of blood surfaced from an almost imperceptible[49] cut on her cheek.

"Such a pretty face," Charlie admired. "Who would have guessed she was capable of committing such an ugly crime as murder?"

Albert's body trembled with anger and confusion. He looked into the eyes of Miss Lovely, also trembling, and begged her to tell him it was all a lie. But she couldn't. Because then it would be a lie.

"Albert," she wept. "I'm sorry. I never meant for *this* to happen. I thought she was already dead. They told me she was already dead! And I just had to push her in and dispose of the body, and if I didn't, they would frame me — they'd destroy me, they said, and my son, too, and I'd go to jail and — and — and I didn't mean to, Albert. Everything just got so out of control. I wish I could take it all back. But I can't. I can't. And I'm sorry. Really. I'm really, really sorry."

"Oh, shut up!" Principal Klinger barked like a drill sergeant. "You are not sorry. You did mean to. You knew exactly what you were doing, Laura. Exactly! Now, would you like to tell him why? Or shall I?"

Miss Lovely's head and shoulders bowed under the heavy burden that was hers to bear. Biting at her bottom lip, she closed her eyes and sighed. "I needed a job." Her voice subdued. "I needed the money. I have a family to take care of. A son — a son just like you."

Her mind reflected back to his birth and early childhood; to days once happy, now marred by terrible storm; a storm she could have avoided had she but heeded the warnings. Long streaks of mascara trickled down her rosy cheeks like rain down a window. Her mouth filled with the bitter taste of salt.

"I'm sorry," she apologized for her sudden burst of emotion. "He just means so much to me. And they were going to take him away — for good — because I didn't have any income. I was desperate, Albert. And selfish. I wasn't thinking about anything else. I just wanted to take care of him like I was supposed to. I just wanted him to be happy again... like he used to be."

"Oh, boo hoo hoo!" Principal Klinger mocked, dotting at the invisible tears in his eyes. "We all have family, Laura. Or," he looked at Albert, "we all once *had* family. Who cares? Get over it. What's done is done. You didn't have to take the job. But you did. So you can't blame anyone but yourself. You see, Albert, Miss Lovely here came to me with her resume, but it was not nearly good enough — not for the prestigious[50] Elderwood

Elementary anyway. She said she really needed the job though. She'd do anything, she said. Anything. So I made her an offer. Help push Ms. Hogsteen into the ocean and the job is yours. And she accepted. Good thing too or we would have had to use one of Sideburns' more painful methods of persuasion."

Laura buried her head in her hands. "I was going tell you, Albert. I was going to turn myself in. Them, too!" She pointed at the Klingers, at Big Cheeks and Sideburns and Veronica. "You have to believe me."

Charlie raised his hand. "Oh, I believe you, Laura. Which is precisely why you are tied to that chair." Removing his knife from the wall, he stepped over to a nearby desk and grabbed a book from its top drawer. It was the black one from the library. "Lovely, lovely Miss Lovely. Did you really think you'd get away with it? Did you really think I wouldn't put things together? Please. I was plotting attack strategies in the bush before you were in the Kindergarten. Who else would have stolen it from my office? I must admit though you showed criminal promise, sneaking behind my back like that; planting it in the library; encouraging *him* to do his history report on a real cowboy; hoping he'd find it and take it to the police and save the day. You could've been one of Al Godón's best, Laura. Instead, you're his scapegoat." He ran the back of his fingers across her neck, then up her cheek. "Pity he's not here to meet you. He might've spared your life to temp as one of his servants. Or maybe you could've worked as a saloon girl for my brother over there, eh?"

Miss Lovely turned away, red with offense and mortification[51]. She looked at Albert and forced a smile. It was faint. But it was sincere. "I'm sorry. I tried to tell you. In the library, I tried. But you ran away."

"Tragic," Principal Klinger remarked. "It seems someone in your family, boy, is always running away. Only cowards run away. You should know that by now."

Albert gritted his teeth. "I hate you. I hate you all."

"Don't hate us. That fat old cow got what she got because of you."

"What?"

"Her job was to keep snot-nosed kids like you from daydreaming. But she failed. In spite of her, you daydreamed even more."

"You just couldn't stop," Big Cheeks' gravelly voice butted in. "Could you?" He took the mouthpiece from around his neck and fastened it onto the trumpet. "You had to follow your sad-excuse-for-a-partner everywhere. Everywhere! Across Death Valley and onto the streets of Dead Dog Crick, into the saloon and behind the counter, down the stairs and into the secret basement — our basement," he thumped his chest, "where you eavesdropped on our secret plans and forced us to stop production and cost me my paycheck!"

Without warning, Big Cheeks swung at Albert, missing his face. Immediately, his heavy hand cocked back for a second try.

"Stop!" PJ rocked back in his chair, slamming its legs onto the floor. "Leave him alone. He din't do anything."

"Shut up!" Big Cheeks thundered. "He took off from Dead Dog — not you cowboy! You were stupid and came back. He's the one who wanted to play hide and seek."

"But I wasn't hiding," Albert tried to explain. "I was daydreaming, and I got in trouble, and —."

"No excuses!" Big Cheeks retaliated. "Partners don't travel alone, kid. But PJ over there was alone. What else are we supposed to think you were doing? Don't even try to tell me you didn't run to get help."

Albert shook his head, but nothing more. It was clear to him their minds were made up.

"This is a cruel world you live in, boy. Deal with it. There are consequences for actions that can't be escaped. Ms. Hogsteen learned that the hard way. Now you and your partners over there will learn the same lesson."

"No!" Albert cried. "You can't do this."

"And why not?" Charlie asked, tightening his pony tail as he stepped across the room, stopping in front of Albert. "Don't worry, soldier. It'll all be over before you can say *Missing In Action*. And if you relax, you really won't feel a thing. Now," he checked his watch, "I didn't dodge bullets to waste time killing a measly sixth grader. So let's get on with it."

Snapping his fingers, The Colonel Principal directed Sideburns and Veronica to the farthest corner at the back of the room. "Bring it all," he said. "Every last particle."

They did. Stepping back out of the shadows, they pushed a metallic cart to the forefront of the room and removed its cover.

Albert gasped. PJ and Laura, too.

Piled atop the upper tray, like a massive volcano of impending death and destruction, was a prodigious[52] pile of powder; a delicate, white powder — like...

"Chalk dust," Principal Klinger whispered with eerie delight. "Chalk. Dust."

27

THE RESCUE

Principal Klinger grabbed a handful of the chalk dust. Like sand through an hourglass, it slipped through his fingers, settling back into the pile on the cart below. Albert swallowed the lump in his throat. His time was running out.

As a baby so easily slips in and out of sleep, so his mind did with time. Like friends on a playground, past and present intermingled before his eyes. He remembered the many happy days of his childhood but then the many sad ones, too. He thought of his mom and his dad. He thought of PJ, and Miss Lovely, and Joey Kornwallace and how he had said that sometimes you can't wait for things to happen; how sometimes you need to make things happen — because if you don't they might not ever happen at all.

Albert closed his eyes. He had to do something. Deep down inside, where he rarely allowed himself to go, he knew that it was up to him, and whatever that something was, he had to do it now. For Joey. For PJ. For everyone.

Albert jumped to his feet and ran. Immediately lowering his shoulder, he slammed into his principal, knocking him to the floor. Like a deer over brush, he went hurdling over the heap of army-green and raced for the door.

"Yeeehaw!" PJ shouted, ignoring the burn from the ropes about him. "Run for it, partner. Go! Go! Go! Go!"

"Get him!" Charlie commanded from the floor.

"Run Albert!" Laura cried out. "For all of us, please run!"

Albert sped ahead. His tiny legs were pumping faster than they ever had before, yet he could still hear someone closing in on him.

"Run!" PJ yelled again. "Faster!"

"Look out!" Laura screamed. "Big Cheeks is behind you!"

But Albert didn't dare look back. Arms outstretched, fingers reaching, he continued to run for the doorway. It was his only chance to escape. But then — *Bang!* — he stopped; his hand inches from the doorknob; seconds away from freedom. A trail of smoke split the room in two. Ears ringing, Albert slowly glanced over his shoulder, and it was then that he saw the bullet hole dotting the wall. But it was not near him at all; rather, it was a thumb-length away from PJ's head. It was a warning.

"I's din't haveta miss." Sideburns cocked both six-shooters and turned them again on PJ; one aimed at his heart, the other at his head. "If you's open that door," he warned Albert, "your partner dies."

Veronica waltzed in front of Laura. "And your teacher, too." She hiked up her dress and removed a shiny black pistol from a frilly red garter around her thigh. She cocked it — *ch-chook* — then kissed Miss Lovely's forehead with the tip of the barrel.

PJ looked right at Albert, his face made stern by the gravity of the situation. "Partner. You listen to me now, you hear?"

Albert sniffled that he did.

"Don'tchya worry 'bout us. You run for it now. You get away, and you don't ever look back."

"Please Albert," Miss Lovely pleaded. "Run. We'll be fine."

Sideburns blew at his moustache, his lips trembling. "I's said slowly step away from that door, boy!"

"Don'tchya do it, partner. Run! Go on now! Get outta here!"

Albert closed his eyes. In outright defiance, his head shook back and forth. "Partners," he cried aloud, "don't leave partners behind." Dropping his hands, he turned away from the door. "I'm sorry," he whispered to PJ. "I won't leave you."

Big Cheeks immediately grabbed Albert and forced him into a chair at the center of the room. Wild Willy stepped over to his brother and helped him to his feet.

"How touching," he remarked. "Your loyalty to that sad traitor will be the death of you. Are you really prepared to die? Just to stay with him?"

Albert wiped his eyes but said nothing.

"So be it."

"No!" PJ protested. "Kill me in his place. It's me you want. Me! C'mon. Look at me! Look at me! Gosh dangit! Kill me — me, me, me — you no-good, dirty —!"

"Shut up!" Spinning on his heels, Willy aimed his gun and pulled the trigger. A bullet ripped through air, lodging itself deep into PJ's leg, dyeing his chaps red on contact.

PJ lunged forward in pain and screamed. It was a terrible scream. Miss Lovely began to cry. And Albert looked at Willy with a hatred he had never before felt. He opened his mouth to curse their existence, but Sideburns stuffed it with a dirty rag.

"Wise choice, boot," Charlie applauded, grabbing a second handful of chalk dust from the cart. "If you can't say anything nice, don't say anything at all. Didn't your parents ever teach you that? Oh. I'm sorry. I mean your *parent*."

Through his gag, Albert mumbled every bad word he could think of.

"Charming. Miss Lux, please keep him steady."

At The Colonel Principal's command, she moved in front of Albert, so that they were eye to eye.

"Albert," PJ grunted through the pain in his leg. "Look away! Don't look into her eyes."

Albert closed his eyes as tight as he could.

"Yes! That's it! Whatever you do now, keep 'em closed!"

"Shut up!" Willy screamed again.

"If you open them," PJ continued, ignoring Willy's demands, "she can make you do anything she wants. They tricked me, partner. More than once. But you've gotta be better than me. Don't make the same mistakes I did. Whatever you do, don't let them —."

"I — said — shut — up!"

Bang!

Another shot rang out from Willy's gun. A second heart-wrenching scream followed, and Miss Lovely's sobbing grew louder.

"PJ?"

A quiet moan rumbled from behind the cowboy's sealed lips.

"PJ?"

Albert couldn't keep his eyes shut any longer. He had to open them. He had to make sure his partner was okay.

"No!" PJ finally called out to his young friend. "Don't do it, Albert. I'm okay." A mouse-like whimper escaped from his lips, but then it grew and grew into the ferocious roar of a lion. The pain was almost too much. "I'll be fine," he lied to protect his partner. "Please. Just keep 'em closed. Dangit. Please. For me."

Principal Klinger brought his dust-filled hand in front of Albert's face. "You can't keep them closed forever, grunt. If you let me, I can close them for you — for good."

Albert remained silent.

"Very well. Sideburns. As usual, please."

Sideburns stepped up to the chair and cracked his knuckles. Then he jammed his thumbs into Albert's eye sockets and proceeded to wrench his eyelids apart. Albert struggled to keep them closed, but the more he resisted, the harder Sideburns pulled. It felt as if his eyelids were being ripped from his face; as if his skin was stretching and tearing and…

"Aaaagh!"

The pain was too much. He couldn't — keep — them — closed — any — longer!

In an instant, Veronica Lux came into sight. Albert tried to look away, shifting his pupils up and down, to the left and the right—it was no use. She was too close. Her bright eyes pierced his own and, as quick as a wink, he found himself utterly helpless. The white pile of dust on his principal's hand loomed in front of him like a dormant mushroom cloud of death.

"Pity to waste all of this dust, really. There's at least seven or eight good diamonds in here. And Godón knows every one counts."

Charlie pointed to a door across the room which, when opened, revealed hundreds of thousands of sparkling blue diamonds. Albert's glance shifted from the diamonds to the chalk dust in his principal's hand. His mind raced back in time to the room in which he had spent his detention; the secret room full of used chalk boards covered in dust; dust he had spilled on the floor.

'You're spilling the dust,' Klinger had shouted. 'Be more careful,' he had warned. 'Dust can be used for things.' 'Things you wouldn't understand.'

But suddenly, Albert did understand. That's why Elderwood's teachers were always assigning detention to the kids; so they could clean all of those boards; so they could collect all of that dust; so they could make all of these diamonds; so they could afford 'buying out every country.'

"Ah. The light has finally clicked on, has it?" Klinger nodded his head approvingly. "You see, Albert, we learned very early on there wasn't anything we could not buy or control with money.

However, we also learned there wasn't enough money to buy all of the things we wanted, or rather all of the things Al Godón wanted." Charlie picked up a pinch of chalk dust and blew it into the air. "It was just a matter of chemistry, really. It wasn't long before we discovered the means by which to accomplish Al's goals. Our blue diamonds passed every test, allowing us to buy things as we pleased. Peace talks and wars. Allegiances and armies and politics. Economics, audits, sales figures, the stock market booms and the crashes, and, yes, even school curriculum. Math, Science, English... History! Our very pasts, Albert. Because he who controls the past controls the future. Power, Albert! That's what this is really about. Life is a struggle for power. When we try to share; when we try to meet people half way, things fail. But when one — one person exerts total dominance — that's what makes the world go round. Power controls everything, Albert." He looked into the sixth grader's watery eyes with a gleam of respect. "Everything except the imagination, that is. That, I'm afraid, we cannot buy. Nor can we control. Unless, of course," he forced his hand under Albert's nose, "we kill it off entirely."

As if signaled by this last phrase, Big Cheeks picked up his trumpet and placed his lips against the shiny mouthpiece. His cheeks puffed out like giant sails on a pirate ship, and a somber funeral dirge hit the air.

Her job now done, Veronica stepped behind Albert to make room for Principal Klinger to do his.

"Any requests for your tombstone, soldier?"

A muffled cry for mercy squeaked from the rag about Albert's mouth, but nothing more.

"Very well. It's been a pleasure having you in school, Albert. I'm sorry I won't see you next year. Really, I am."

Principal Klinger's hand flattened, settling the dust across his palm like a thick pancake. His lungs filled to capacity, and his eyes narrowed in on the target. Albert could do nothing but watch. Time slowed down, passing as if frame by frame. This was really *it*. The end of the great adventure.

Principal Klinger's eyes closed, and as his cheeks relaxed, a puff of pent-up air came billowing out like a great fog. Millions of particles of chalk dust leaped from his palm. Taking the shape of a giant claw-like hand, they grabbed at Albert's face.

PJ couldn't watch. And he wasn't going to either. With a strength he had never before known, he burst from the fetters that bound him to his chair. Sharp shots of pain exploded through his legs where the bullets remained, but he ignored them all. Jumping from his chair, he ran to Albert, waving his hands in the air, yelling and screaming for Klinger and Veronica and Sideburns to stop.

"You yella-bellied jackal!" he suddenly screamed at Sideburns, an idea for a possible escape forming in his mind. "Yeah *you*! You ugly desert dog! You dirty side-burned oaf! You're — you're — you're nothin' but a dim-witted slow-draw!"

"Slow-draw?" Bubbling over with instant rage, Sideburns let go of Albert's eyes and reached for his six-shooters.

"Albert," PJ immediately yelled, his plan having worked, "now's your chance. Run for it, partner! Run!"

In quick response, Albert pushed off the ground with his feet. His chair tipped backwards, moving away from the oncoming cloud of dust. He was falling...

"Albert!" PJ yelled again. "The chalk dust. Watch out!"

Albert turned his head just as the deadly cloud reached him. Barely brushing his cheek, it sailed over him then into Veronica's eyes.

"Aaaah!" she wailed, slapping the air. "I can't see. I'm blind!"

As she ran away in a daze, Albert's chair crashed to the floor, tossing him head over heels into a wall. He struggled to his knees, looking for PJ, his hero, who was running toward him to save him once and for all —

Bang!

Another shot exploded into the air, this one from Sideburns' gun. Albert screamed as his partner stumbled forward, grabbing his thigh again. But then, to Albert's relief, PJ quickly regained his balance and, straightening his stance, continued forward determined as ever a cowboy was.

It was going to take more than a couple of bullets in the legs to stop him from saving his partner this time. Because, he reminded himself, that is what real cowboys do best.

As Albert watched his partner struggle forward, it was all he could do to keep from shouting for joy. He was going to be rescued! They were going to escape! They were going to go home! If you just put your mind to it, he squealed inside, there was, indeed, always a way —

Bang!

Another trail of gun smoke swirled through the air. This time, PJ fell to his knees, grasping at a red stain in the center of his stomach. He looked at Albert. 'Don't worry,' his glassy eyes seemed to say. 'Me and you, me and you. Partners. Forever.'

But a third shot and then a fourth ripped into his plaid shirt. He doubled over, clutching his heart. His cowboy hat fell to the ground. Instantly, tears of pain welled up in his eyes, blurring the image of his hat; the one thing he felt represented him more than anything else in the whole world. Why, it made him who he was. It was his reputation. In its brim were his strength and his courage. It was his last hope. And he had to keep it on… But as he reached out to grab it, his shaky fingers managed only to brush its side, and the whole of it shifted forward — just beyond his reach.

Sideburns raised his gun again and cocked it. With no other choice, PJ abandoned his hat, hoping The-Golden-Spurred-Man-Upstairs would understand. Rising to his feet, he looked Sideburns square in the eyes.

"You can't kill us," his voice shook. "We were partners once. Partners!" He thumped his chest. "And so help me, we'll be partners again."

Bang!

A fifth and final shot exploded from the silver barrel in Sideburns' hand. PJ's body jerked backwards; his neck quivered and his eyes closed; then, quite subtly, a gentle smile spread across his face — as if he had been relieved of a heavy burden — and his body crashed to the floor. A small puddle of blood immediately formed, trickling out from underneath PJ.

Albert screamed. He jumped to his feet and ran for his partner, but Charlie dove for him first, grabbing him by the ankles, taking him down. He gripped his army knife and raised it over Albert's head.

"Help!" Albert shouted, kicking at the knife. "Help me! Please! I need help!"

In answer to his plea, the door smashed open and in rushed a glorious ray of light. "The game's up!" Albert heard a man yell. "You're through!" Then: "Albert?"

Albert looked around. Hundreds of officers stormed into the room.

"Police! Police! Hands on your heads! Hands on your heads!"

The criminals opened fire. But the law returned it. Screams and shouting pierced the air. Albert looked around again, desperately trying to find the man who had called his name, but he couldn't see a thing. Smoke filled the air. Bodies darted back and forth.

"Albert?" he heard his name called again.

"PJ?"

Freed from her ropes, Miss Lovely broke from her chair. She ran to PJ's side and threw her body over his, protecting him from further harm. With grateful tears, she kissed his forehead

over and over and over again. "Patrick," she cried. "Come back, Patrick. I'm sorry!"

Sideburns ran up from behind Albert and grabbed him. He jammed a gun under his chin. "Any closer and the kid dies." Saliva dripped from his mouth as if he was sick with rabies.

"Help! Help me! Please!"

Albert heard someone yell his name yet again, but this time the voice was louder. Sideburns turned sharply on his heels, his guns blazing. In a blur of action, the silhouette of a man dove through the air, knocking Sideburns and Albert to the ground. A sharp pain screamed inside Albert's head. The taste of blood filled his mouth. Beside him, a fist fight began. The two men rolled around, swinging at each other like savage beasts. Albert couldn't tell who was winning.

Willy ran by, grasping at his stomach. "I'm hit," he gurgled. "I'm down."

Then Big Cheeks fell too, the chain about his neck snapping as he crashed to the floor.

With improved vision, Veronica winked at the officers as fast as she could but to no avail. It took four cops, but in the end they threw her against the wall, tied a blindfold about her eyes, and cuffed her hands.

Charlie braced himself behind a chair. Relying on his experience in the war to protect him, he fired off rounds like there was no tomorrow. But even with all his experience, he was no match for the men in blue. Two shots were fired. First his shoulder. Then his thigh. He was down! And with that, he raised his hands in the air.

"I dodged bullets so you could be a cop!" he shouted at the men applying the handcuffs. "Show some respect!"

All the while, the fight next to Albert raged on. It was fast. It was furious. And then, all of a sudden, it was deadly. A heavy stain darkened the cement. It was over.

Overcome, Albert dropped his head to the floor, and his eyes went black. He tried to move, but he just didn't have the strength anymore; his body and heart and mind were spent. For what seemed like hours, he lay there, trying to catch his breath, listening to the noises around him soften; listening for someone to tell him *they* had won. And then he heard it; from not-too-far-away, like a snore, but louder; someone was breathing — heavily. Footsteps *tapped* over the cement. Then a comforting shadow fell across his small, quivering body.

"It's me," a man whispered. "I'm here, partner."

Albert's body was bruised and sore, but upon hearing the familiar voice, all pain melted away. Through tear-filled eyes he raised his head and looked at *the man* in front of him. It wasn't one of the criminals. It wasn't a policeman. And it wasn't PJ, either. It was even better. Better than he could have ever dreamed of. Better than he could have ever imagined.

It was *him*.

The man bent down and scooped Albert up in his arms, cradling him close to his chest.

"It's me," he whispered again. "I'm here for you, son. I love you," he choked. "I love you. Now, let's go home."

"Dad?" Albert's voice trembled for joy. "Dad? How'd — how'd you get here?"

Albert's dad looked deep into his son's eyes and smiled. "You," he said, pausing to wipe the grateful tears from his eyes. "You brought me here, Albert. You. I'll always be here for you, son. Sure as shootin'. For sure, for sure."

28

A Partner Returns – for Good

High in the periwinkle blue sky, the sun burned like a giant orange on fire. Perched outside Albert's window, a family of birds chirped in unison. Inside, the house was quiet.

Albert sat at the kitchen table drawing a picture of a cowboy and his bronco. His mom placed a cookie sheet in the oven and set the timer. Taking a seat beside her son, she took his hand in hers. She smiled. He turned to her and smiled back. She rustled his hair with her other hand and laughed. Together, they sat there lost in silent but happy conversation.

Then the doorbell rang.

Her head tilting to the side, she motioned for Albert to go. Leaping from his chair, he raced to the front room.

"He's back!" he shouted. "He's back!"

But when he opened the door, it was not who he expected to see at all. A strange man in a fine grey suit stood on the porch. He smiled at Albert as he set his briefcase down on the steps.

"Albert McTweed?" the man asked with a thick east-coast accent.

Albert nodded. His mom stepped around the corner.

"Ma'am." The man tipped his hat and handed her the morning's paper from the porch. "Pardon the intrusion. I had to see *him* for myself." His hand shot from his side and grabbed Albert's. He shook it vigorously, then harder still. "Son," he said kind of misty-eyed, "I'm real grateful to you for all you've done. I know my brother Thaddeus P. would be grateful, too." His eyes glanced to the sky. "May he rest in peace."

Albert's mom put her arm around her son. "Uh... mister?" she kindly interrupted. "I'm afraid you must have the wrong house."

"No, ma'am," he said returning her kind smile. "The McTweed residence, I presume?"

"Yes..."

"I apologize if I've caused you any concern or confusion. Allow me to introduce myself. The name's Zookenowski, Bartholomew T. Attorney at law. Like," he paused, looking at the sky again, "my good brother before me. Just flew in from New York. Big criminal case here. I'm sure you are aware of it." He smiled at Albert again. "I'm going to lay down the law." He pounded a fist into his palm. "Bring the mighty sword of justice upon their heads and avenge my good brother's good name. Our practice, too. We were partners, you know?"

"Thank you," Albert's mom said out of courtesy. "I think that'll be enough. We are expecting someone, though. Any second now. I wish you luck with your case."

Bartholomew tipped his hat again. "I understand. I won't be taking any more of your time. I know it's precious." He bent down and picked up his briefcase. "Albert," he said, shaking his hand again. "It's been a real pleasure. If you ever need my services..." He reached into his pocket, withdrew a card, and handed it to him. "You just give me a call. Any time — day or night. Ma'am, thank you for your time. You have a great boy there."

He then turned to leave, but got no further than the last step before he stopped and turned around.

"Oh. I almost forgot. I thought you might want this, Albert. Picked it up off the warehouse floor right before I came here to see you. I have enough evidence anyway. Don't think the cops will really mind."

Anxious, Albert watched as the man reached again into his suit pocket and withdrew a shiny, golden chain. Dangling from it was an even shinier trumpet mouthpiece.

Albert's eyes expanded with excitement and disbelief. In the medallion's reflection, he could see himself — as clear as day — his smile big and bright, like the sun. He looked back at the lawyer, who tipped his hat as if to say 'Good job' before walking down the driveway and slipping into his car.

Albert's mom closed the door, quickly leading Albert back toward the kitchen.

"What was that all about?" she asked. "Peculiar man. Don't you think? I'm sure he had the wrong house. What's that he gave you?"

Albert looked at his smiling reflection in the golden medallion then shrugged his shoulders. He had made a promise not to tell.

'She'll worry,' his dad had said. 'This'll be our little secret.'

And it was.

"Very strange," his mom said again. "And what was that about the morning's paper? And a big criminal case? He definitely had the wrong house."

The oven's timer buzzed and Albert's mom stepped into the kitchen and removed the pan.

"Chocolate chip," she smiled. "Nice and hot."

Albert sat back down at the table. He grabbed a cookie and ate it, then poured a tall glass of milk. He looked out the window. The daylight was as bright as it had ever been. And he was happy. So happy, in fact, he didn't notice two things.

The first being a fresh batch of chocolate chip cookies almost always meant something bad had happened, or something bad was about to happen; and the second being a shiny black car which slowly pulled up in front of his house and stopped. The passenger window rolled down. A Hispanic man with a scar on his face and a tuft of cotton in his lapel looked at the house. A devious smile formed. Then the window rolled up, the driver was signaled, and the car pulled away.

"What's taking your dad so long?" Albert's mom wondered aloud, anxiously tapping the table.

Albert shrugged his shoulders again, then grabbed another cookie and dipped it in his milk. His mother rolled the rubber band from the newspaper and spread the front page out across the table to take a quick gander at the daily headlines.

And then she gasped. "Oh my."

Epilogue

The school year at Elderwood Elementary (the best school in the whole world!) ended as it began — with the ringing of a bell. Sweet liberty! And summer break, like flowers after lots of rain and sun, was in full bloom.

Having successfully passed the sixth grade, Albert E. McTweed resolved never to look back; though that is not to say reality trumped imagination. In fact, for Albert, quite the opposite was true; his powerful imagination continued to blossom just the same, the ambiguous[53] line between reality and imagination but a shaky stroke drawn into a dirt floor, over which the characters in his life—both real and imagined—continued to cross from time to time. Through the simple medium of his daydreams, he found the courage to not only look his problems square in the eyes, but work his way through them. And in doing so, he was never alone again. Within his dreams, the people who loved him most found him; and in that same special place, he found them, too. In the end, however, he was simply excited to start junior high. And that was all that really mattered.

Bartholomew T. Zookenowski was true to his promise. The mighty sword of vengeance did, indeed, fall — hard — and in the midst of a national spotlight.

In a stirring turn of courtroom events, old cases were re-opened, new proofs submitted, and both Charlie and Willy Klinger were found guilty of the murder of their parents, as well as a great many more misdeeds. Upon their release from the hospital, they were escorted to jail where Charlie was forced to trade in his army-greens for prison-orange.

Big Cheeks also went to prison, but without his trumpet. Void of any opportunity to exercise his cheeks, they turned flabby and now hang down around his shoulders.

Al Godón, the elusive criminal mastermind behind *everything*, remains elusive and at-large. No one knows just when or where he will next appear. Vicarious[54] crime continues to keep him safe from the long arm of the law. Almost daily, someone takes the fall on his behalf. Such is the life of a mob boss.

BLUE DIAMOND COTTON, INC., however, was not so lucky. After filing for bankruptcy, it shut down for three months while it underwent audit and reconfiguration. When it finally re-opened, it did so under new ownership and a new name: Buckin' Bronco Cotton Company — on account of the bucking bronco they found tied outside the company gate. *Buckin' Bronco Cotton*, went the new slogan. *The Toughest Cotton on Earth. For the Cowboy in All of Us.*

New records were not set that quarter, but the company did see a steady growth in sales. Albert's dad was not a part of that team. The greatest cotton clothes salesman this side of the M-i-ss-i-ss-i-pp-i found another job... closer to home. As did one hundred or so other excellent workers, who, after testifying against their criminal employer, turned in their blue smocks and fake diamond recipes and returned to Mexico.

Veronica Lux spent but two nights in prison before convincing the prison guard on duty to remove her blindfold and let her go. He claimed he didn't know what he was doing at the time.

"Her eyes," he kept muttering. "Her eyes, her eyes, her eyes."

He was placed on probation and required to visit a psychologist two times a week. At the present time, Veronica roams free.

Do keep your eyes closed.

Sideburns Magraw was flown to a nearby hospital so his injuries could be properly treated, but took his own life that same night after mistaking the doctor's intentions. His last words, the befuddled doctor told police, were: "You's ain't gonna *shoot* me's. I's a can do it my's-self."

Bang!

After several days of failed attempts, Ms. Hogsteen's body was finally recovered. It took two cranes to pull her up from the ocean floor. Having no kin, the heavy-heavy weight division of the World Wrestling Association generously paid for the two burial plots needed, requesting, as compensation, the entire funeral be televised. It was.

As for Miss Lovely, the judge had mercy on her. To everyone's relief — especially her son's — she walked away from the courtroom without sentence. After a semester on unpaid leave, she was allowed back at Elderwood Elementary — full-time. She currently presides as principal. Her first act of leadership was the immediate dismissal (just a pink slip this time) of Ms. Pistol and the just-as-immediate disposal of all chalkboards, which were replaced by dry-erase boards and markers — much to the delight of the marker-sniffers.

Joey Kornwallace and PJ McDougal were buried side by side. Joey in a new Cub Scout uniform, all badges restored; and PJ with his hat, boots, and spurs. The service was beautiful. I believe cowboy heaven's population is one more than it was the day before. And if there's a Cub Scout heaven, surely the same holds true. No doubt, it was a happy reunion for PJ and the true love of his life when they saw each other for the first time after so many years apart. After all, absence, they say, makes the heart grow fonder.

And lastly, we come to Albert's parents, Laura and Patrick James McTweed. As you may have surmised[55], or at the very least hoped, they did indeed work out their differences. Whatever those differences were is not important. Sometimes in life we just lose sight of what is important. That is all. It doesn't make any of us bad guys. It makes us human. And being human, we have the chance to correct our mistakes; we have the opportunity to start again and be better than we were yesterday; we have the freedom to choose the world in which we live. At any time we so desire, we can pack up our bags, throw them on the back of our bucking bronco and head home.

Home. It's where you hang your cowboy hat. And it does not get any more real than that.

Sure as shootin'. For sure, for sure.

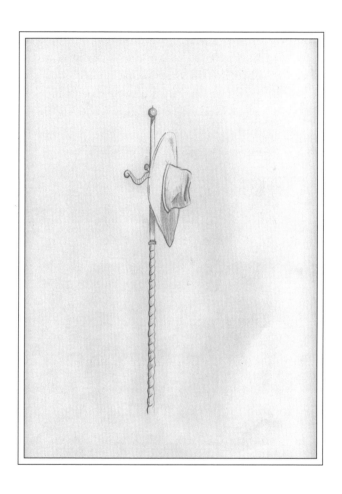

The End

Glossary

Printable version available on
WWW.ARTHURTLEE.COM

1. **Burgeoning:** To grow or develop rapidly.
2. **Whistle Dixie:** Any one of several songs with this name, popular as a Confederate war song during the Civil War; to indulge in unrealistic and optimistic fantasies.
3. **Just deserts:** An outcome in which virtue triumphs over vice, good over evil. (Often pronounced just *desserts*).
4. **Miscreant:** Villainous, evil; heretical.
5. **Shroud:** A veil; blanket; covering.
6. **San Andreas fault:** A major geological fault located in California; the source of serious earthquakes.
7. **Ignominious:** Deserving disgrace or shame; degrading; dishonorable.
8. **Catacomb:** A burial ground.
9. **Caustic:** Capable of burning, corroding, dissolving, or eating away by chemical action.
10. **Chortled:** To chuckle gleefully; a snorting, joyful laugh.
11. **Credulous:** Showing a lack of judgment or experience; naïve, gullible, believing.
12. **Dirge:** A funeral hymn or lament; a slow, mournful, musical composition.

13 **Reverberation:** An echolike force or effect; a repercussion.
14 **Nefarious:** Evil or villainous; infamous, atrocious.
15 **Fortitude:** Mental and emotional strength in facing difficulty, adversity, danger, or temptation courageously.
16 **Bravado:** A pretense of courage; a false show of bravery.
17 **Enigma:** Anything that arouses curiosity or perplexes because it is unexplained, inexplicable, or secret; a mystery.
18 **Euphoria:** A strong feeling of happiness, or well-being; sometimes leads to overconfidence.
19 **Smidgeon:** A very small amount, scarcely detectable; a bit.
20 **Retrospection:** The act or process of surveying, reviewing, or contemplating things in the past.
21 **Agitation:** Extreme emotional disturbance; not calm.
22 **Foliage:** Plant leaves, especially tree leaves, considered as a group; a cluster of leaves.
23 **Cryptically:** Mysterious in meaning; puzzling, ambiguous; involving or using code.
24 **Stifled:** To suppress, curb, or withhold; to cut short.
25 **Catalyst:** A person or thing that causes an event or change.
26 **Intonations:** Intoned utterances; a manner of producing tones; the use of changing pitch in one's voice to convey information or meaning.
27 **Whimsical:** Determined by chance, or impulse, or whim rather than by necessity or reason.
28 **Brackish:** Distasteful; unpleasant.
29 **Privy:** Made a participant in knowledge of something that is private or secret.
30 **Malleable:** Capable of being shaped or formed by hammering or pressure from rollers; impressionable.
31 **Oblivion:** The state of forgetting; official disregard or overlooking of offenses; pardon, amnesty.
32 **Vaquero:** Spanish for cowboy; commonly pronounced "buckaroo" in old western movies.

33 **Inaudible:** Impossible to be heard; not loud or clear.
34 **Raiment:** Clothing; garments.
35 **Aspirations:** The act of breathing in; inhalation; a strong desire for achievement; ambition.
36 **Jury-rigged:** To assemble quickly or from whatever is at hand for temporary use; makeshift. (Often pronounced *jerry*-rigged).
37 **Meandering:** To move aimlessly and idly without fixed direction.
38 **Lesions:** A wound or injury.
39 **Diatribe:** A bitter, sharp, or abusive denunciation, attack, or criticism.
40 **Traverse:** To pass or move over, along, or through.
41 **Chafing:** To make sore by rubbing; to irritate or annoy.
42 **Nay-sayer:** A person who expresses negative or pessimistic views.
43 **Wrest:** To take away by force; jerk away by a violent twist.
44 **Opaque:** Not shining or bright; dark; dull; stupid or unintelligent.
45 **Drag-rider:** The cowboy who follows the herd of cattle, pushing the stragglers. Incidentally, the drag-rider has nothing to look at but the backsides of the cows.
46 **Floozy:** (*Slang*) A gaudily dressed, usually immoral, woman.
47 **Insinuation:** An indirect suggestion or hint, especially of a derogatory or mean-spirited nature.
48 **Audacity:** Boldness or daring, especially with confidence or disregard for personal safety, conventional thought, or other restrictions; (slang) guts.
49 **Imperceptible:** Very slight, gradual, or barely noticeable.
50 **Prestigious:** Having a high reputation; honored; esteemed.
51 **Mortification:** A feeling of humiliation or shame.
52 **Prodigious:** Abnormal; monstrous; extraordinary in size, amount, or force.

53 **Ambiguous:** Open to or having several possible meanings or interpretations; difficult to comprehend or distinguish; lacking clearness or definiteness; indistinct.
54 **Vicarious:** Performed, received, or suffered in place of another; a substitute.
55 **Surmised:** To think or guess without certain or strong evidence.

COME! SEE WHAT'S ON

WWW.ARTHURTLEE.COM

For kids and adults, students and teachers— FOR EVERYONE!

Reading guides
Chapter quizzes
Printable glossary
Writing exercises from *The Daily Muse*
Critique Sessions at *The Critics' Corner*
Works in progress
Author biography
Questions and Answers
Polls and Contests
…And more!

I HOPE TO SEE YOU THERE… IN YOUR COTTON COMFORT WEAR!

ARTHUR T. LEE

 started writing creatively when he was six years old. His first book, a one-page story entitled *The Rainbow Goes to Japan,* was chosen by his first grade teacher to go to the local Young Author's Conference. Says he, "It was clear to me then—while on the swings at recess, I believe—that writing was what I wanted…yearned…*had* to do." With several more Middle Grade and Young Adult novels in the works, Arthur currently resides with his wife and three boys in Washington state, where, he says, "I have the privilege of telling my kids a bedtime story each and every night."

Visit Arthur at www.arthurtlee.com.